THERE IS NOTHING STRANGE is Susan Pepper Robbins'
third book to be published. Her first, 'OneWay Home' was
published by Random House in 1993, and 'Nothing But The
Weather', a collection of short stories, was published in 2014 by
Unsolicited Press. Susan has been published in many journals,
and won both the Deep South Prize and the Virginia Prize. She
lives in Virginia and teaches at Hampden-Sydney College.

THERE IS NOTHING STRANGE

Susan Pepper Robbins

Holland House

Paperback ISBN 978-1-910688-04-5
Epub 978-1-910688-05-2

Cover Photograph by W. E. Pepper, Jr.

Cover design by Ken Dawson Creative Covers:
www.ccovers.co.uk

Typeset by handebooks.co.uk

Published in the USA and UK

Holland House Books
Holland House
47 Greenham Road
Newbury, Berkshire RG14 7HY
United Kingdom

www.hhousebooks.com

FOR OLIVER, REMI, COURTNEY AND THOMAS

CHAPTER ONE

Weldon has just put his arms down and is holding hands with himself behind his back and doing some kind of shimmy, pelvically close to Liz McClellan.

He's good, no doubt about it, and she can keep up with him for now, but only on this rented temporary dance floor that came on a truck, folded in three layers with steel hinges.

The band appreciates his dancing. Weldon hopes Rebecca is watching, which she is, and so is Martha Travis, his current girl friend. Everyone is watching. The Brightleys are here at the wedding reception, not dancing, deliberately not thinking of Kelly who would have been the bride's age next month. Laura invited them, and to Rebecca and Weldon's surprise they came. After eight years, the Brightleys have reached this stage of grief: being able not to think of Kelly for certain periods, up to as long as three hours, and they can soften the ways she returns to them.

Dead children continue to grow, keeping up with their friends as they graduate and marry. As a break, for relief, Alma Brightley has learned to think that Kelly is away, couldn't make it home for some occasion, this wedding, for instance. Alma can think in great detail about Kelly's activities as a twenty-two year old woman—away on a trip, preparing to return when she has taken care of some business, a sale, matters several states away, a trip involving airports and layovers. Or on a long vacation where there are so many interesting things to do; there is no time to call. Or graduate school. Or some small problem in her own married life just begun.

But now this bride, holding a beer can in her left hand, turns, bends, and reaches down behind herself to scoop up an armload of air in the lacy train with her right hand, then moves out from the tent into the warm rain, toward the groom who is almost as drunk as he was the night two years ago when he took the fraternity pledges and stood on the railroad tracks signaling the roaring Chesapeake and Ohio, "Come on, come on. Hit me, hit me, Choo Choo."

Laura, Weldon and Rebecca Cauthorn's daughter, has just married her first husband—that's what the one-armed best man, Henry Moorefield, calls the groom, Jeremy Hill. Laura's first husband.

Two years ago, Henry lost his right arm, stretching it out in the furious wind the train made. Now, the accident is water under the bridge, but married for twenty minutes, Jeremy has the same expression on his face that he had that night: that hit-me-you're-so-fucking- big-try-it-you-damned-stupid-idiot-train.

Laura loves the set of Jeremy's eyes daring the coming train, his arms up and open, waiting for the full-court press. That gesture. It says "I'm ready, I hope you are because when you hit me, you will be sorry."

Laura has explained to Rebecca why she must marry Jeremy. The expression, the open arms, the indifference to dangers. She must marry a man who dares trains to hit him, who loves her that much. There is more to it than she can say, but she is hopeful. She is the bride.

She thinks that Rebecca should feel the same pure hope for her reconstituted marriage, for Weldon, her recovering husband, and should be more appreciative of the possibilities that the dangers of their lives can engender, produce, manufacture, ignite. Laura's advice to her mother is to leap toward dangers and then work with the fallout. When Rebecca says that she did feel exactly such hope and disregard once, and repeats that she did feel that hope for many things not just once but often in her marriage to Weldon, and goes on to say that trains have hit her and Weldon, that trains do hit people, that one almost killed Jeremy and Henry, Laura rushes in with "Yes, yes." But still it is clear that Rebecca does not understand what Laura means by hoping against hope, hoping in spite of facts, hoping, as the song goes, when all hope is gone. Hope is really, Laura says, an assertion of the self against the universe. She does not sound exactly like the self-help gurus on TV and radio, but not altogether different either. Great effort creates hope, the key ingredient to miracles. We can be happy, if, and only if, we kill ourselves trying. Laura's got it figured.

Laura hates for her mother to state the obvious about terrible events or even imply it or allude to the facts of their lives—the long separation, the infidelities, the drinking, the debts, Weldon's implication in the death of Kelly Brightley, the failing health of Weldon's mother, and it breaks Rebecca's heart for Laura to miss the point in spite of the many ways Rebecca has of phrasing it: Love fails, people change, circumstances cohere and accelerate, conspire and explode in accidents, casual infidelities occur just like that, meaningless except for the certain urgency to the participants not to the left-out person, hearts break, minds collapse, people die.

Everyone in the world knows these facts, and Laura does, of course, but she thinks there is more, much more to be said about them and to be done about them to change them or redirect them. Such facts can be, if not exactly overcome, and not overlooked, but dissolved in the hope that is just waiting to be released, to unfurl and fly—something along those lines.

Laura knows a lot, and so does Henry, but it seems to Rebecca as if they ignore some basics. A lost arm, for one thing.

No one knows what Jeremy knows about love. Young, handsome, hard working, ready smile, he might know more than he lets on, but he acts as if knowing is not his problem; he's doing his part, he's the one getting married. To hell with knowing. He's an action man. He has had three jobs to finance his new life, catering, lawn maintenance and fire wood deliveries. Even with these jobs, he is deep in debt for the liberal arts degree which is not worth the paper it's on, he laughs, adding that at least it got him Laura, the wife he wanted, the wife of wives. He has been working since he was fourteen, but hey, he says, his old man started working at nine, riding in the trucks of a plumber so he learned everything and would have his own business by now except that he made some bad decisions. Don't ask him anything, Jeremy has told Laura who plans to ask everything. Now Jeremy works all the same jobs he had in college, but "with panache" because now he's a graduate.

"With panache." Jeremy apologizes for using a dumbass Henry-phrase, knowing that Henry likes to see his influence on his rival. The job market reality has hit Jeremy at a higher level now that he's been graduated, but he has met the challenge, kept right on with the teenage jobs he can do in his sleep. But with panache. He can debone a chicken with his bare hands, no knife, shake out baskets of fries with one hand and flip burgers with the other. He delivered fire wood all through high school. Unloaded a truck in town before eight in the morning; made another delivery after school. "Good with my hands," he likes to say. Can bushwack and Weed Eat acres of poison oak, can landscape landfills, can and does keep his dad's 1939 Chevy Business Coup running, and has parked it in the yard for the wedding, not that it will be the car that takes him and his bride on their wedding trip, but "just because" and also because Henry's mother said he could park on the grass. She seemed to understand it as a statement about this groom, this wedding at her home. The car says something about Jeremy who is a find, a gem, a great guy with his short hair and work ethic, a dream boat, a gambler who is betting on his own strength of will and purpose and today in his tuxedo he looks like a river boat gambler from an old TV show.

Alma and Hill Brightley are looking at him, sizing him up, weighing him and knowing that he's Kelly's type too.

Rebecca has heard Laura tell the story of Jeremy's dare to the fraternity boys—Henry leading the pledges—dozens of times. The coming roar, the shouted instructions, the darkness; then the confusion and shouts for help and to God. Jeremy's heroic work to save Henry. Henry's courage. Laura's helpless horror as she stood in the dark watching. From that moment, Laura was bound to Henry in a different way. Henry, everyone knew because he told it, was in love with her. Jeremy, though, was the person Laura loved, wanted to marry, to live with forever.

These are the simple mysteries, the facts that are at work at the September wedding.

Rebecca studies Jeremy for his eligibilities which are obvious, (handsome, ambitious) but in this situation demand scrutiny, emphasis. Henry has said that if the train-thing is the deciding factor, then Laura should be marrying *him* today. After all, he is the one, the winner of the train tourney.

"My arm, well, uh, my stump." He lifts it to the sky defiantly, indifferent to its comic, foreshortened gesture. "I am the one who lost an arm that night. I am the real groom here, the best man, literally speaking. No offense." He says this without a flicker of anything like aggrandizement, self-pity, false heroism, bitterness, even courage. Just simple fact. He took the dare, welcomed the train; his arms were out, ready. He stared, he set his eyes at the rushing freight train. He was the one. He loves Laura that much. And how did loving Laura get mixed up in the fraternity dare? Somehow, it did because young men not all that far removed from their boyhoods were involved, willing and able, ready. Waiting for a train of some kind to roar at them and then pass by into the night, leaving them feeling much better.

Henry reasoned thusly: If Laura were hooked up with the president of the fraternity, the one who organized the train thing, then she well might turn her attention to a man who did it better, took the train on, took it down. You know, did it better, was better.

So, Henry is lovingly skeptical of Laura's explanation of her marriage, her locomotive love theory. He won that night, jousting on the tracks. He should get the lady, not just her scarf or ribbon, her friendship or whatever. Those are nice, but not worth squat when one considers the big cheese. Laura's way of choosing her husband is laughable, "risible" he says, too loose, too broad; it encompasses small multitudes of grooms, at least all the fraternity pledges of that year who stared at the coming train, not as fiercely nor with anywhere near the abandon of the stout, two-armed Henry Moorefield, but still, there were others in the field.... Any one of those young men would love to be in Jeremy's shoes today. But Henry, who is drunk now, keeps saying he's the real one, the right one, the one-armed, loving, proven man. He is, he insists, the real groom. The winner. It is almost out of hand, his behavior, but who you gonna call? People don't hire off-duty policemen for afternoon country weddings in Virginia.

Henry is saying to small groups of people that they cannot forget the dark sisters in the cave, snip-snipping and spin-spinning threads. This wedding is not important in the big picture, the long run, not a problem. Fate will take care of things, not to worry. Carry on.

After the accident, the fraternity was barred by court order from coming within fifteen yards of the tracks, so Laura's choices, by her own fiat, for grooms are limited to those men. No more train fights, no more man-against-the-machine, no more fighting the coming of the industrial revolution with sheer spirit and body, those glory days like others are gone. The Greek system, houses, pledging, all that prolonged adolescence, and thank god for extending it for him, are gone with the wind.

And then, Henry returns to his theme: Laura made the wrong choice from those suitors. He makes his way around the crowd, working it as if he were running a campaign for the House of Delegates.

The fraternity boys were not, of course, all suitors. They have their own girl friends who are at the wedding, the bridesmaids, laughing and drinking beer. Everything fits together: the bridesmaids and the groomsmen are matched. Perfection personified, Henry says and then, "Count them," Henry points to them. "Three beauties, three graces: Katlin, Jennifer and Claire, Laura's support group, they will get her through this terrible day." These girls have their lives ready and waiting for them. They were graduated in May. Katlin, computers. Jennifer, her own sandwich shop, and Claire is teaching middle school in downtown Richmond, where statistically, they all expect her to be murdered either in her classroom by an older fifth-grader or on the playground in a drive-by. Henry points out that the dangerous job enhances Claire's appeal, already considerable. The bridesmaids don't mind if their dates sing in harmony, "We all love Laura" to the tune of something old like "In the Gloaming" or "Beautiful Dreamer." In fact, they join in.

The Brightleys are watching, not wounded that Kelly is not there because in a way, she is.

The bridesmaids understand Henry's loving Laura and, to an extent, what is going on here. Henry talks about it enough, and they are so familiar with the story. It's true that Laura was the only one of them who saw the accident, and she was not supposed to be there. It was a secret initiation ceremony, one Jeremy knew about from an alumnus who had come back for Homecoming. Laura went, saw it and since then, Henry has been even more *there*, joined at the hips—Laura's and Jeremy's. It's a little sick they agree, but what can they do?

"This choice of a groom is only a temporary decision," Henry is saying, and then adds, "necessary but temporary."

There is a slanting air to the wedding as if the sky had loosened and come off its hook at one corner and a tattered section were brushing across all of them at the wedding.

The wrong groom for the bride—that story, old as the hills. But everyone is married to the wrong person in some ways, and always there are wrong things, missing things, aren't there? It's life. For example, there is the absent Kelly, though her parents feel her hovering and acknowledged.

Rebecca and Weldon, the mother and father of the bride: at odds for years, but today coming closer, circling each other at this wondrous occasion, their gift to Laura—reconciliation has come just in time for the wedding. Hell or high water, her words. Weldon says all men are different but all husbands are the same, and that is the problem he has with marriage—being both man and husband, he has it tough, but will do his damnedest and needs all the help he can get to heal this breach between the individual and the state, this contradiction of man-husband. Diversion or drink has been helpful, very. He admits he has gone too far with both. He likes to say he can't be both man and husband at one time, but he can try as he is trying to be one after the other, to take it sequentially, and it's husband time now and will be until they lie down for the last time in their graves. Incompatible, the two beasts—man and husband. He wants to be a good husband, but to date, it has not been possible. He tells the truth, says these things and is believed. He loves Rebecca and that should be enough. He married her, didn't he? Marriage is marriage, but life is life. Martha Travis and Liz McClellan are hold-overs from his old habits of having at least two women lined up, half-ready for something to happen, a move on Weldon's part that this time he is serious.

And so, Weldon, father of the bride, and Henry, the best man, have something in common about the way they see themselves in the sexual universe, only Henry is a quarter of a century behind Weldon but believes anachronistically, medievally, or is it an obsessed, stalking way, that there is one person, "and that would be Laura," he says, on earth for him to love. He will love her any way he can, as a friend now, perforce, and only later—he must accept it—as a husband. Something, God willing, may happen to Jeremy, probably only an early divorce, but there are other possibilities that will remove him from the picture.

For Henry, it is love, the real thing, you can believe him. Jeremy will have to watch his back, psychologically speaking. It cannot hold that Laura will continue to love or stay married to Jeremy.

Weldon knows about this kind of passion, but applies it severally, liberally, to the string of women—three is a string, he keeps as insurance. At present, there are three women who appreciate the music of love he can dance to. Martha over there and Liz, there. Rebecca, the long-suffering wife too. To his face, the good Republicans call him Bill, but are too kind to call Rebecca Hillary.

"Right?" Henry laughs, reading Rebecca's anxieties, and picks her up with one arm, a kind of sling hug, the mother of the bride, "but not my bride, yet" he whispers to Rebecca, and dances her around in the same music that Weldon and Liz McClellan are dancing in as Martha Travis watches. At the farthest tip of Henry's swing, Rebecca's hand slips, and Henry, unable to use his other arm, the missing one, to reach out and grab her fingers, watches Rebecca twirl and spin off, lower and lower so that in no time, she has fallen and is spread eagle, her skirt billowing down on the floor. Hands reach down to pick her up, she's righted and propped, brushed and patted. Everyone laughs.

Rebecca hears Laura saying, "A grown woman falling

down dancing! That's my mom." Proud of her, laughing and helping her up with her sympathetic arms making upward sweeps, Laura is perfection. She wants her mother to try dancing a wild fandango with Henry now, to try anything. The fall was a good first move. Rebecca stops dancing, but Henry won't, and he goes on, bending at the waist, doing that thing with his shoulders, holding up his one arm and waving it, all by himself. Megan, his date— "That's another story" Henry likes to say, when anyone asks about Megan who is always aware of Henry, where he is, what he's saying, what he's doing and who is with him— will see him in a minute and come over, dip her shoulder and pick up the beat a few bars away from where Rebecca left off. Megan refused to be a bridesmaid, and got out of it without offending Laura or Henry. She can manage her own miracles, a few a day, especially if Henry is involved.

Rebecca has splinters in the heel of her hand where she hit and skidded on the dance floor. Laura has come over to her and is holding her mother's hand and asking Jeremy to go in the house and ask Mr Moorefield for some witch hazel.

"Some what?"

"You heard me, New Husband!" Laura kisses Jeremy.

"Did you have the wrong groom at your wedding, O Mother of the Beautiful Laura? Is this history repeating itself?" Henry asks Rebecca later under the music when she has let Laura pour witch hazel on her hand and Megan has lifted out the splinters and said, "Good as new."

Then Rebecca goes back, dancing with Henry and Megan now. They are upright, dancing, not flung apart and jerking and circling the way she had been dancing with Henry before she crashed.

Henry knows the Rebecca-Weldon history—who doesn't at this wedding—but he thinks, as Laura wants him to, that Weldon is perfect, that any problem originates in Rebecca, though she is in a way perfect too. Being willing and able to take the blame is yet another perfection that is still to come. "Still, the one," Henry sings as if he knew who would have to be blameworthy.

"It's becoming," Weldon has said, "the way blame rests on Rebecca. I want all young women to learn that traditional grace, but without the traditional punishments that enforce it—if this is not asking too much. Grace may be genetic or a given, not something achieved." Henry and Weldon express themselves in similar ways and to everyone. Another reason for his being the right man for Laura, the best one, the man who is very like her father except for the women thing. Henry has not told Weldon this plan for Laura and him, the assumption that Jeremy will disappear, but he will.

"Later," he says to Megan who has heard it all before and has her own agenda.

During the reception, Laura holds Henry's left hand, and comforts him, tells him again, maybe, that he was only a sophomore when they met, one of the pledges, a year behind Jeremy and, actually, two behind her—almost a whole generation measured in college years. She can marry a man a year younger, as she is. Jeremy. But come on, two years is getting into the older woman thing.

"Later," he says.

Henry has doubled up his course load and is ready to graduate in December, a semester early, and at twenty, just the age Laura was when she graduated. All this effort to prove he's not that young. Laura seems anxious about him keeps his hand deep in the folds of her gown. She is gripping it hard.

Rebecca loves to watch Laura with people—always holding their hands, explaining what has happened and that everything will work out. She breaks out in hives sometimes, watching Laura, but she can't stop. For one thing, Laura is beautiful. People say she was born beautiful and therefore will have only certain kinds of problems. And if Laura hears herself being discussed, will enter into the talk, and add her two cents. "It's not easy," she will laugh when someone lifts her hair that is unbelievable the way it's dark, but reflects blue and red running electrical lights. But it, Laura's life, looks easy. Love is simple, Laura will say earnestly if the talk turns from beauty to love, as if she were a maiden in a ballad, about to die of true love and fertilize a briar rose from her grave. She would love hearing that and laugh her loud laugh that sounds like a call, a high HOOO with a GH to round it off as it drops a note.

She stretches herself out to touch people at her wedding because they are there, yes! Barbara and Dwight, Sally and Lewis, Fred and Roxanne, Chris and Ginger, Mr Waters in the wheelchair and Mr Harrell, not in one yet at ninety-seven. Trey and Andrew, Phil Turnbull, Alice and Jim, Mrs. Anderson and MacKenzie! Thank you for coming she says with every gesture. It's too hot for you out here, "way too hot," come stand by this big fan.

Laura had gotten Jeremy to set fans around in the tents to stir up some air and with the threatening rain in the ninety-five degree heat, they stand and feel the breezes unsticking dresses and shirts from legs and backs.

Won't she spread herself too thin trying to fix the world, get things back in order on the shelf she has in her mind?

Alma Brightly watching Laura lets that question float across her mind, recalling Kelly's still impossible room, untouched, still needing to be picked up, the shirts and jeans draped and thrown, unwashed, waiting.

Rebecca has seen Laura rehang cups on their hooks so they have the same flowers facing out because she did not want the cups upset. When Rebecca had said, "Oh Laura, don't be crazy," she had smiled and then cried. "I want things right, even if it's only cups, only stupid stuff. Don't think I haven't read everything about controlling types, all that."

Laura is strolling across the lawn in the mist steaming up from the grass in the lulls between rains, taking a swallow from her beer, touching everyone as they open up a path for her. She will interrupt a conversation to hug someone and say "I love you."

Who can resist that direct assault? There are dead soldiers everywhere at the wedding. Hugged and told they were loved by the bride, they fall, ennobled. Megan, too, is embraced, forgiven for her unrequited love for Henry, and loved more.

What will happen to so much love, Rebecca wants to ask Laura who would tell her that if there were time and they were anywhere other than at Laura's wedding, that love flows out into the world turning even cups hanging in the cupboard to their best sides. Loving is different from controlling. It's that hope thing she has talked about. She would laugh and hug her difficult mother who falls down, who can't dance, and who refuses to live with her husband full-time, the one she has not divorced, so isn't that proof of what Laura is saying?

Laura throws herself back against the air when she

laughs, trusting it to catch her, lifting her silver beer can high as she seems to fall but does not. Someone has said something that Laura makes into something better, something interesting. "You can't mean that you said *that* to her!" Then the wedding guest bobs and nods with more spirit, "Yes, Yes, really, I did, word for word. You can believe me."

Martha Travis has won many points in her effort to capture Weldon by listening to Laura and agreeing with her. But Rebecca is sure Laura has explained to Martha the hard truth that a mother is always a mother, even a Martha Travis with all her appeal is not the mother, *Laura's* mother, not Rebecca Cauthorn. Laura has gone into the story of the long labor, the C-section, the failed Lamaze that Rebecca had, that Weldon coached, that brought forth Laura. Martha Travis hangs on the words. What choice does she have?

Laura offers sympathy, smiling at this point about her mother, maybe ruefully, apologetically to Martha. When people have trouble understanding Laura's points, she comes at them from another direction, trying to make them see what she means. Henry will step in to interpret for Laura sometimes as in this: "Weldon may dally with a Martha and a Liz, but dalliance is not matrimony. Nor is a Martha or a Liz a Rebecca." Then he adds for his own benefit that a wedding is not a marriage.

Still, Martha Travis and Liz McClellan are here at Laura's wedding. Weldon dances first with one and then the other. And Rebecca is here too. Twenty-two years married to Weldon, another wrong groom, not always married in any ordinary meaning of the word, she is, more or less with Weldon today, September fourteenth. They drove in two cars, but together. A first date after another separation in their marriage.

Laura's love for Jeremy must not be, of course, as simple in its origins as Laura claims—the train—and Henry will not accept what she has to say about her choice of groom. He pushes her away, removes his hand from the folds of her dress and stands up. She rises with him, wanting to explain to him again that his love for her is, in fact, something else. She would like to hold his hand a little longer and look at him, but he pulls her into his semi-embrace. They are the same height exactly, and in her heels she may be a little taller.

She should be marrying him. That, he grips Laura's shoulder, is the simple fact of the matter. Here he waves his left arm at the guests, the flowers, the tents—all this is all a big mistake. Remember (he does not have to say this so he does not) that he had been doing exactly what Jeremy, the then-president of the fraternity, was doing, only doing it better. Of course, he was doing it, exactly, insanely, worse. Too damn close to the train, too drunk, too damn crazy, trying to be a little better than Jeremy, showing his willingness to enter into the pledging spirit. Henry simply says the wedding is a mistake as he dances, checks on people's drinks, talks and laughs.

Losing an arm, he lost Laura. That's what some people think, but it may not be the case. Henry insists that his arm and this wedding are only temporary losses, setbacks. Megan listens, familiar with the whole story.

Weldon is sorry that Laura did not marry Henry. First of all, it seems that Henry understands Weldon—maybe not the love life, but the basics; then there is the Moorefield family's lost money and residual sense of themselves as monied, a sense which is for Weldon as important as the actual money because it is his own condition; then there is Henry's appreciation of Laura and by extension, all women when she is not available or when she insists on marrying someone else. Add to these affinities Henry's deep ambivalence about careers, then locate everything here at this beautiful old place called "Whitfield" in New Kent County, the home of Henry's parents who insisted on it. Did they, in fact, insist on having the wedding here, as Henry said they had? And how could parents of a best man insist on this? But, anyway, Henry is perfect for Laura which means perfect for Weldon.

But, Rebecca keeps saying to herself, it is Jeremy Hill who is the groom. And, Megan is thinking, thank you, sky, trees and rain, for the fact that Jeremy Hill has just married Laura.

Jeremy broke down and cried at the altar, the one that he and Henry had built. He cried. Exhausted by his three jobs and by cleaning up the honeysuckle bank at the Moorefields', this Jeremy who fought trains, cried. No one knew what to do, so they all waited. Jeremy blew his nose, coughed, looked up at the sky—it was just beginning to rain—and they saw his face stretch into weeping. It could have been mistaken for a wide grin, but the sounds were those of a man crying. His head was lowered, his shoulders trembled. His mother walked up and put a handkerchief in his hand and that's when he blew his nose and the vows went on. He loves Laura too.

"Of course he does," Henry said and meant it.

Everyone has heard the story of the train accident so many times from Laura and Henry. Jeremy does not relish it the way Laura and Henry do—nor does Megan—or like the boys who were there that night and now, to a man, are at the wedding.

Weldon tells it as if he had been there. It goes like this: Henry steps up onto the gravel slope to the tracks, and being high on an afternoon's worth of six-packs and some illegal substance, leans and sways on the small embankment broken by creosoted ties. He sees or thinks he hears Jeremy's clothes rattling ahead and to the right of him, that is to say, closer to the tracks than Henry is, in the hot wind made by the speeding train. To Henry, the imagined sound of the snapping shirt was, he has told Weldon, like the sound of flags, medieval ones, rallying him to things braver, so he crouched and banked on the gravel, a skier, his arms in front of him but steering in swoops closer and closer on his cross-country run. Of course, he could not have heard Jeremy's cotton shirt flapping in the wind in the roar of the train.

One exasperated counselor at the college suggested that what Henry had heard was his own empty sleeve, pre-flapping, trying to warn him to get away from the tracks. His sixth sense was saying "Get Back, Get Away, You Will Lose Your Arm. You May Be KILLED." He had violated his own safety mechanism by stepping up into the train's path. The counselor urged him to listen to that sixth sense more carefully from that point on, having been given a second chance.

Henry says now that he had another intuition that night—feel free to call it a vision—that Laura, who was standing in the dark trees, tall and dark herself, almost invisible except, he says, to him who saw the reflectors on her white running shoes glinting, Laura loved what was going on at the train tracks. And Henry wanted whatever

it was she loved, "Oh yes," he will pound the table like a
bad actor, and mutter like a worn-out traveler home from
the wars and deep in his cups, "I loved Laura the moment
I saw her with my bonny blue een, as who could not, and
I would have done anything. Know what I'm saying? That
night at the tracks, I fell in love. More than I was already, I
mean. If Laura had stepped from that grove of beech trees
in her reflecting, bright shoes to suggest that she would
enjoy watching someone, someone named Henry perhaps,
catch that train, scramble to the top, then run backwards
along the spine of the cars leaping across the dark air
between the cars like an expensive stunt man, I would have
done it. No problem.

"So, when I saw that Laura would marry Jeremy in spite
of my having lost my right arm in manly competition, as
it were, in spite of my being, at least, train-wise, the better
man, I decided to outdo my best friend Jeremy, yes he is my
best friend in all other ways, his bride being the one mote
in the eye of our friendship, as many ways as I humanly or
sub humanly could." Henry lifts one eyebrow and laughs
his demon lover laugh that everyone, especially Weldon,
loves to hear. Yes, he has admitted, the fact of losing Laura
was "disheartening, but in an enriching way, a way that
gave his life even more meaning—if painful meaning."

Henry was the right one for Laura. Weldon is sure of this
and has told Rebecca and repeats what Laura has explained
to him about why she chose Jeremy, an explanation that
gets hung up in the train story. "Implicit, can't you see
it," Weldon will end, irritated with Rebecca's deliberate
blankness.

Henry understands himself, he will tell you. He is a
senior psychology major. Ask him anything about the dark

side of competition, the friendly act of murder which is often necessary, he says, in order to win a point. He has at last understood that Jeremy had him beat in a way he could not make up for—age. Jeremy was older the night of the train, Jeremy was the one leading the men to the tracks, the one who was going first to show them how to take the charge only because he was older than Henry. Those college years and always forever thereafter, Jeremy was, is and will be the older one. Read Sulloway on age-orders.

Suddenly when these thoughts about time occur, Henry will strike up (his words) Shakespeare's Sonnet 123 to drive back these downers that suggest that he is helpless and must change his mind about loving Laura, must accept facts.

> *"No, Time, thou shalt not boast that I do change:*
> *Thy pyramids built up with newer might.*
> *To me are nothing novel, nothing strange;*
> *Da Dah, Da Dah, Et Cetera, Et Cetera*
> *This I do vow, and this shall ever be,*
> *I will be true, despite thy scythe and thee.*

And so, da-dahing and cha-ching, Henry declaims, *"Time can be conquered by love such as mine."*

He has told Jeremy and Laura that when men reach their early-to-mid-to-late-thirties, the distinctions in age disappear for a decade, time enough for him to win Laura away from Jeremy. Henry, by then, will be in his late twenties, just the age that women, he has read, like men to be. The assumption that he must cause devastation, a divorce at the very least, is so obvious that it does not bear mentioning.

Jeremy suggests that Henry may have to lose his other arm. To which Henry gives his eloquent shrug, and smiles,

"Whatever, it takes."

Even in the hospital, Henry said that his left arm met the challenge. Only the right arm—and he did have two, so what was the deal everyone was talking about—got taken, captured.

Henry would not let his father file a suit against Jeremy, or the college, or the fraternity, or the Chesapeake and Ohio. He pointed out that insurance was paying for everything, even a long rehab, not mentioning that there had been prosthetic sessions which he skipped as if they were history classes on the siege of Charleston in 1780.

When he got out of the hospital, there were court-assigned group sessions. In spite of Henry's not allowing his father to sue, the police had charged Henry with reckless endangerment, and the judge ordered the classes on peer pressure and risk taking for Jeremy and Henry. Laura would drop them off at the court building because the judge took away their drivers' licenses and they couldn't drive to the classes themselves (though they drove everywhere else). Completely illegal, Henry's mother said, meaning the classes and the revoking of the licenses, but who, she said, would argue with a judge who was an alumnus and probably had himself done things like stand by the trains.

Henry now has his tux sleeve pinned up like a Confederate vet, and is dancing his heart out on the tented yard where on April 25, 1861, the Black Eagle, Company E of the 18th Regiment, Virginia Infantry was mustered. The yard will be Henry's if he can pay off the mortgage. His family had insisted in a bewildered way—just following orders, Rebecca suspected—when they offered Laura the sloping lawn on the river for her wedding. The honeysuckle could be cut back. Henry swore that his parents had begged him to offer Laura "Whitfield," the lawn at least, and the caterers were welcome to use the kitchen, the guests the bathrooms, yes, his parents had begged him, Henry crossed his heart, fell on his knees, offered to cut his wrists ("Well, the left one") swore and swore, that he was simply conveying their wish, their hope that Henry's friends would use their home for the wedding.

"To get ready for ours," Henry said looking at Laura his arm around Jeremy's shoulders.

Laura had accepted the offer because, as she explained, she did not have a home with parents there from which to have the wedding meaning a mother who would stay married, stay at home. Weldon and his mother, Gram, who was eighty-three, could not put on a wedding. The fact was, Laura said, her own mother would not come home to give her a wedding, so thank God for Henry's parents. The wedding would be at the Moorefields' "Whitfield" in New Kent, and so the invitations went flying out from the Moorefields' address, a post office box they got for the occasion to avoid having "Whitfield" on the envelope, though it was on the invitation.

Henry blossomed after he lost his right arm. For the first time, he made dean's list, then was elected president of the student body. Now he tells everyone that peer pressure saved his life, faster than Jesus, he says. He traded his arm for his new life. A fellowship is waiting for him for graduate work in divinity, maybe law, his professors tell him. Psych majors can go on in anything. Henry appreciates what Jeremy did for him and says that Jeremy will continue to bless him. No one doubts his meaning.

Henry's volubility smells of bourbon even when he's not

drinking; in that way, he's much more the 1963 fraternity man than he is a "nineties kind of guy." Weldon is Virginia '61 and appreciates Henry's capacities for liquor and what he calls the finer things. There is no X-generation in Henry; in fact, he claims he doesn't know what it means.

But, facts are facts, and Henry is dancing at Laura's wedding with the bride, who has just married Jeremy Hill. Weldon is not dancing with Martha Travis but with Liz McClellan so that Rebecca will be confused, which she is not. She is trying to move beyond her old self (the trees) and see what Laura wants her to (the forest). And deep down Weldon hopes that Rebecca is straight about the dancing, but he goes through the motions of diversionary flirtation so, he will tell her later, his girl friends will be happy. They want to be discreet around his wife even if she is not quite a wife, more like an adjunct wife—attached but not really there—a wife on a date.

Weldon teaches history part-time at the local community college—it's been eight years now. Everything is divided into full-time and part-time, the sacred (part-time) and the profane (full-time), appearance (full-time) and reality (part-time), childhood (full-time) and adulthood (part-time), sex (part-time) and death (full-time). Weldon thinks dividing the world this way helps him.

Henry tells everyone Laura chose the better man, for now, the one with two arms, the one with a degree in hand. It's cool. Fine. Bride material is everywhere. Plenty more of bridal fodder in this wide world, and ready he is, he says, and willing are they. He grabs Megan who is handy and they spin off.

Megan's parents, George and Marie Marshall, are there. They are part of Weldon and Rebecca's old crowd insofar as they have an old crowd and their daughter Megan is the mirror image, that is, the exact opposite of Laura, but the two girls went off to college together—not as best friends, but friends. Megan is straight A's, a track star, forensics ace, wound as tight as a spool of wire. Megan's parents bought lake property, one of the economic initiatives/ventures the county made in the early eighties. The cottage on the lake was the Byrd sisters' 1927 sprawling "retreat." The Marshalls have not sold out as most of the lake people have done by now, and they have bought the restaurant at the courthouse to keep the cash flow flowing they say and to keep faith in the community. The county appreciates the Marshalls' efforts to support the lake project, even though no native speaking Rivannan would buy a lot on the lake. They do go to the Marshalls' restaurant. It's a renovated old country store with glass-headed gasoline pumps, a hand-worked cash register and a deli. Sometimes there is an art show of water colors, photographs, or Christmas ornaments.

Girls fit Henry better now that he's without an arm; there are sexual advantages he says, licking his chops as he glues Megan to him, her head level with his shoulder, her left arm tight around him. She is a friend, he says, she is Laura's friend, and she loves Henry, but unlike Laura, she wants to marry him. Can't be helped, Henry seems to say.

The trouble is the old one: Hook, line and sinker, "totally" Megan says making fun of the right word for her hopeless love for Henry. Corrects it with "Immersion complete." Laura requires a retinue as Weldon does and it helps to have Megan and her bleeding heart around.

Inverting his sentences shows Henry's independence from the X-generation and the grunges. Back-assed sentences make people pay more attention to him. He is one of those five-foot eleven men, one of those wired men, coiled and ready, the ones tall women love, the ones no one believes they will leave their husbands and young children for. Megan is short and perfect. She has said that she will marry Henry when Laura makes him available. "Release Me" is one of Henry's favorite—he says "fav-oh-RITE" country songs. Megan has told Rebecca with tears welling in her eyes that Laura has resisted Henry for reasons no one understands.

"It *is* a mystery," Henry will add, shaking his red curls, and "As my second fav-oh-RITE country song says, 'There's a First Time for Ever-thang.'" He says first marriages are part of the maturation process, and he has accepted it. Megan Marshall, petite, perfect, beautiful as a miniature Persian painting, outlined in gold, knower of computer languages—she has just learned Oracle—agrees, looking at Henry sadly, then over at Rebecca.

Megan dances with Weldon and listens to him tell her how happy he will be in his marriage from now on. Weldon espouses and advocates renewed improved marriages.

And so, Laura Cauthorn, Rebecca and Weldon's beautiful daughter, has married Jeremy Hill on the lawn of the family of the man who loves her. It is true that she has danced all during college with Henry while Jeremy took care of fraternity business or was working at least three jobs. And it was Henry who drove the black Thunderbird convertible, left for twenty years in a barn on his parents' farm, around the stadium with Laura, a Homecoming Princess sitting on the top of the back seat in a blood-red angora suit with a huge corsage of white chrysanthemums, a wound reversed, he pointed out. It was Henry who advised

Laura when it was time to declare her major (English) and about piling up student loans (don't worry, don't transfer to a state school, you'll lose credits and net-working potential, plus it's worth staying put because we will be together because I am here for you, to advise you, whatever), and about her parents' long-but-not-that-unfriendly separation (don't interfere, parents are beyond help), and Laura's persistent yeast infection.

It was Henry who first conveyed to Rebecca the crux of Laura's problem: Her mother had ruined her life. You have to watch mothers. They can kill you without meaning to. Very dangerous people. Mothers not fathers. By leaving Weldon so often and for so long, Rebecca had made Laura take on responsibilities too early: in a word, had made Laura her father's wife.

When Rebecca tries to answer Henry and therefore Laura, as she has tried to since that afternoon in the Marshalls' restaurant, he holds his finger (left hand) up to his lips, "Shhhhhh, it's not your turn. You will get a turn and all in good time. This is Laura's deepest and darkest view. Do not hurt the messenger. I bring you news that is salutary, that will, we hope, help all of us."

Once Rebecca said to Weldon that Henry knew too much about all of them. Weldon looked puzzled, then asked if she didn't think that a future son-in-law should know all that he could about his bride's family.

Henry tells everyone that Laura will see the light at some time in the not-too-distant future, and then she will divorce Jeremy. There will be joint custody of their daughters—Henry has their names chosen, Anne and Emma, from his favorite novels. Henry will not insist on the names, but he will recommend them accompanied with gifts of thousand dollar savings accounts, and then he will read selections from the novels and serve champagne to the expectant parents.

Henry knows that Anne and Emma will have to make some adjustment when they have to stop calling him Uncle Henry and change to Pop or Step-Dad or Harry. He has many of the foreseeable problems worked out. Again, his psych major will come into play.

Jeremy has heard it all. Weldon enjoys these plans because they ring true and seem by comparison to simplify his problems. He is, he says, in his first marriage still and all of the problems are on-going as Weldon and Laura see them because Rebecca is the on-going problem. The only good thing about the situation is that Rebecca has their attention and hopes that she can think of some way to use it to help them all, even Weldon. If Rebecca's father were alive, he would say the only way to help Weldon Cauthorn would be to shoot him, if a bullet could find him.

Laura rolls her eyes hearing the custody story. Henry loves to watch her eyes and says so, elaborating on the allergy shots the unborn Anne will face, the Ritalin the unborn Emma will have prescribed. How he will arrange for a math and Latin tutor for Emma who will be too spoiled to study hard stuff.

"When land is gone and money spent/Then learning is most excellent," he intones, dismissing the values of homework for Emma and Anne. He will provide the land, the river farm he will inherit with its mortgages. More details plucked from the future; more rolling of eyes: more love generated.

Laura's running across the grass in her peau de soir slippers in the gray rain, her train looped over one arm and the beer held to balance the arm with the train is not lost on Henry and not on Jeremy either who loves Laura in a straight-forward, friendly way.

"Normal" he tells Henry. "Two-armed." He thinks that Henry is too complicated for anyone to put up with for too long. No one, not Laura, Jeremy is certain, could ever marry Henry. He watches Henry offering his thoughts to their friends about the beer can and wedding dress. All that talk would drive a person into the ground.

"See the coming together of opposites here on the lawn in the silver rain, an oxymoron brought to life before our eyes, men," Henry says to the groomsmen, all veterans of that night at the tracks. They look, good brothers all, at Laura running toward Jeremy, contradicting all of Henry's love and plans. Henry continues to point out opposing but beauteous things and implies that a bride will turn perforce toward the best man, not now, but later. They are all slightly drunk and very happy to be listening to what Henry says. They remember that Henry has taught them to drive in one lane, the far left at all times, on principle, and to do ninety as often as possible. Why? Because they are young, and it is their only chance. "Buckle up," he tells them, "always." With his left arm, he reaches across his chest to grab the invisible seat belt and pulls it down to snap into place.

He answers implicit questions before they rise into words. "No, I am not planning adultery. My up-coming marriage to Laura Cauthorn, my young friends, is woven into the very fabric, the tapestry of this occasion.

"Some day, in the long future," Henry is up on one of the rented tables now, swaying and bending at the knees, "you will be attending my wedding, my marriage to that same lovely bride here on this same lawn. See her walking through the pearly rain, holding her train up off the wet grass. At my wedding, of course, she will be an older woman, by at least eight, maybe even ten years, worldly, sophisticated in matters of the heart, and thus heart-sore but not ruined by the failure of her first marriage. Her daughters, the Emma and Anne you have heard me speak of, will attend their mother in hand-made dresses, piped and smocked in France. No, Laura will not wear the same gown. For that wedding, she will wear a simpler dress, a grey, that's with an "e," men, British spelling, a chiffon, and will be carrying pale yellow roses, drooping, as even now the beer can in her tapered fingers is tilting."

Henry will not be more specific than this about the failure of the marriage and the soreness of the bride's heart. He concentrates on the festivities of the second wedding. His candor about the bride for that occasion is well matched by his delicacy and sense of the present occasion. The attentive groomsmen, Sean, Thomas and Dewey, nod wisely, drunkenly, ready in the future to stand up for Henry as they have for Jeremy. Henry has given his right arm for them, but it was Jeremy's idea to reach out to touch the train. They will certainly rent tuxes and dance no matter what else is going on in their lives. The bar exam, the CPA exam, residencies, whatever. The bridesmaids are not as willing to listen to talk about a second wedding at the first, but they appreciate and envy Laura's having someone in the wings, someone she is close to already, someone she does not have to look for or meet by chance.

Megan has drunk a bottle of champagne and waits for Henry to come help her catch the bouquet.

Jeremy would stand—Laura has just bet her life on

it—waving the rushing train toward him, and now that they are married, toward both of them. Their college debts come to over sixty thousand for them both, English/psych majors who have not found real jobs. They figure they will have to make at least twenty thousand each, starting. They do not have any interviews lined up.

It upsets Laura that Rebecca and Weldon are only dating, if that is the word, for the "first" time again. They are not serious, and that is impossible for Laura to understand. She has been keeping house for her father and her grandmother, who naturally at eighty-three has "gone back" some, especially after Rebecca left for more-or-less good. Laura has come home to Weldon and Gram on weekends away from her life with Jeremy and Henry and after college her life in Richmond. It would be a nice wedding gift to her if Rebecca would only step in for Laura with Weldon, take the burden of his sadness (a person does not have to look sad to be sad) off her shoulders, help with Gram's increasing frailty, and let them be a family again. This middle-aged dating is a delaying tactic on her mother's part, as Laura sees it.

Rebecca wants to try, but lifting Weldon's spirits takes a tempered steel-mesh spirit, and there are her own spirits hanging in damp paper bags to consider.

Rebecca has tried to explain that it's one thing to be Weldon's daughter, a tall and beautiful young woman marrying a Jeremy, whose life is beginning, and it is another to be the wife, afraid to be in love any longer with Weldon whose entourage includes this year Martha Travis and Liz McClellan. Rebecca is tempted to return to Gram. Who wouldn't be? Gram has loved her as if she were her own daughter. She made their lives possible for as long as her strength held, but now she has announced that she is failing.

"I am going on," she smiles.

That night on the tracks, after the train had passed blowing its whistle, Henry had staggered up, holding his arm across his chest like his lacrosse stick, the hand pointing up, palm out, all wrong.

Henry is, everyone agrees because of his arm, entitled to his plans for Laura who encourages him. His plans are harmless and gild her wedding day.

"Make me a poultice—not the right word," Henry had said to Jeremy who ran, not back along the track where Henry thought he had seen him or heard his shirt snapping in the wind, but up from the path alongside the embankment. Even at that moment with the blood swelling and pumping across the span from his heart to the torn elbow, Henry was in charge. Jeremy had done as Henry directed him, his voice getting fainter and fainter. Ripped off his sweat shirt and jeans, then tied them around Henry's shoulders, a body wrap, almost a tourniquet for the trunk, the whole torso, then the pledges carried him— by then Henry had passed out—in a basket made of their arms to the hospital a mile away. They ran with him in the basket. Jeremy's quick action saved Henry's life. A miracle the doctors said.

In a slow motion now, Jeremy is beckoning Laura over to him. She rushes as much as the dress and the slick grass will let her through the crowd, and when she reaches out for him over the last few steps, he pulls her into his arms.

Henry has been helping the band members snake the cables for the guitars and speakers around the big oak tree to the rigged up set of outlets. When the music starts up again after the break, they will have to wait for Laura and Jeremy to dance, then Jeremy with Rebecca, then Henry will dance with his mother who is trying to be as generous as Henry, to go on with her life as the mother of a one-armed son who does not seem to notice his loss. She wants to follow Henry's lead.

His father has not come out of the house except for the vows. The wedding is terrible for him, it is clear. He sits at the window and looks out at the wedding on his lawn, but he will not come out with the guests. Henry's mother is different. Vivian. Rebecca can feel Vivian's curiosity burning around her but when she comes close to Vivian Moorefield, good manners kill the questions and the two women stand toe to toe, locked in the dead air of aborted conversation. Vivian does not know what to ask and Rebecca cannot help her.

Thank God, they are women and know that some emergency is waiting, that the wedding is a reprieve; being human, they do not know what the emergency is.

Filling the seventeen by thirty-five foot dance floor, rented from the same company that brought the tents and champagne glasses, they will start dancing to the oldies: Shuby Hold On, Aquareeeuss, Kansas City, Standee on the Kournerr, Get a Job (their favorite). Rebecca is popular because she is a version of the bride. People look at her, hold her face in their hands and say, "It's Laura. Can't you see her?"

The bridesmaids, their lives in order, wearing their short, dark purple sheaths with low backs, dance in the mist that settled in after the vows. Megan is clinging to Henry with both arms while he is directing the band with his left arm. Megan's parents are trying not to see what they are seeing.

Henry's mother is glad to see Henry with Megan--maybe he just talks about loving the bride.

No one minds the rain that is beginning to get serious. The tents are sagging with water and Henry will dance around each tent, out in the open, jumping back inside the tent and then straight up to head the sag like a soccer ball, dumping the water in a great waterfall in the place where he had just been dancing. There is applause every time.

Rebecca has on a new rose and aqua silk suit, tea length swirly skirt, and has danced a reserved two-step with Jeremy, and then a wild something with Henry, though not as wild as the dance when she fell down.

Weldon is flirting in an obligatory ways with Liz. Martha Travis and Rebecca are tolerant of Weldon for different reasons: Martha feels hopeful and Rebecca hopeless, but the result for both is tolerance of Weldon. Liz kisses him when the music ends, and stands there as he waves for Laura to come over.

Laura refuses to understand the problems her not exactly-married parents are having on this date to her wedding. They seem dots on the horizon. Martha and Liz are diversions from the real life that Rebecca and Weldon, and his mother, Gram, and Laura—now there are six, counting Jeremy and Henry, have. Laura leaves out the Moorefields and Hills for the time being in her census. She leaves out Megan and the groomsmen.

If Rebecca would come home to stay, if she would only be and stay married to Weldon, Laura would be happy, Gram would be happy. Even Weldon would be happy. Especially Weldon. It's that simple Laura says speaking with an authority granted to an only daughter who is young and beautiful on her wedding day. Rebecca is working on trying to see it Laura's way.

The hills that stretch away from the wedding party are hidden behind the sheets of rain. The guests can see heavier rains moving in. The caterers are beginning to back the panel trucks up to the back door of the house where Vivian Moorefield had grown up, and to load the chafing dishes of seafood and ruined platters of roast beef and ham. Older couples are hurrying toward their cars parked in uneven rows across the field. The Brightleys do not hurry.

Henry and Megan are still dancing, now without the music. Laura and Jeremy have gone, run through the rice-throwing crowd, jumped in the car with tin cans tied behind and disappeared down the drive.

As Rebecca waits for Weldon to go get his car, Henry and Megan dance over to the porch where she is standing. Henry calls up to Rebecca, "Don't worry, Mrs. Cauthorn, my plans may not work out." He is not serious, just polite, considerate. "Some enter at the portal, some do not."

Megan breathes in the air around Henry, rain and all as he looks up at Rebecca on the porch, "I may come, perforce, to see that Laura loves Jeremy and that he loves her. That I am history, a footnote, as it were. Megan here thinks that I may grow up, and that thought has a definite, though limited appeal, as does her faith in me."

They dance away toward the trees.

Chapter Two

The doctors thought for a while that if the antibiotics did not work they were dealing with spinal meningitis. There had been twenty cases in the area. There were the symptoms: Weldon could not bend his head or swallow.

Just after midnight, home from the wedding, Weldon said he was feeling "porous," shot through with malaria or something tropical, and later, at three–thirty, there was a headache that got worse, appearing at first as a simple migraine—but one the Imitrex did not begin to touch.

Giving himself another shot in his thigh, he knew his hands were shaking too hard to give himself a third. A bubble of air, he smiled, "would—sweet—kill me instantly." But then the projectile vomiting stopped his joke. Rebecca got him in the car and to the emergency room an hour away.

As she drove, she could see the future spreading out in front of her on the windshield: widowhood, if that is what it would be called after eight years of separation but no divorce; Laura never speaking to her again for killing Weldon, letting him die the first night of her being officially in residence like the queen, after those eight years. Almost half of Laura's life, Rebecca had stayed away, would not (could not) come home, but had "dated" Weldon. Laura would be sobbing, saying "Then to come home to stay, you promised that you would be starting over, remarrying, on my wedding day, then for you to kill him on my wedding night."

Laura would be standing against a convenient wall,

crying and furious, going on, turning to the wall as if that offered more of a mother than Rebecca, or as Laura would add, more comfort than Rebecca *had* ever offered her daughter. That was not true, but it would not matter in the circumstances.

Obviously planned Laura would say at Weldon's funeral, weeping, weeping: the broken glass of promises, a deliberate fuck up, clearly the worst possible thing that could happen had happened. Henry would be there with them, and would take Rebecca aside to translate Laura's "deliberate fuck–up" into a definition of the way Rebecca had manufactured another crisis so that she could run away from them. Again. He might explain that Laura did not believe in reincarnation of psychological types. Whatever that meant. Not at all, no, Laura was one for changing and healing—balancing of things, of generations, of setting things straight. Her parents' marriage was a sorry thing, but Laura's own would be happy, profiting from her years of studying her parents. She was determined that her marriage to Jeremy would be the very opposite of her parents'—a demonstration of how it's done right. Henry, in stating Laura's marital philosophy, would politely and obviously leave himself out of this analysis. The objective, but supportive counselor, with no vested interest in the outcome.

"I can say that it does seem that you have committed murder, in a way, in a way. Weldon, you have to admit, is dead after all, and that was certainly not in the plan for this September fifteenth." Even Henry would not say such a thing, but he and Laura would think it. Gram would not, and she would be broken hearted.

If Rebecca should yell back to Henry, to Laura, that

she was innocent this time of crisis manufacturing, that Weldon was ill to the point of death on his own, that she was the designated driver, stone innocent–sober, Henry would shrug with a little sympathy, but only a little. He would be acting as Laura's spokesman. "Glad to be of use," he'd smile, rueful, but glad.

Anyway, what is Henry's investment in Rebecca and Weldon's marriage renaissance and rehabilitation? Is it that Laura will be happier? But won't that happiness with her parents' reconciliation redound to Jeremy's credit and add to that new marriage's equity, rather than strengthen Henry's hopes for marrying Laura? Maybe he thinks Laura's happiness will add to *his* credit rating, maybe to his stockpile of arms, maybe to his home page. Rebecca knows she does not understand anything.

And so Rebecca tries to forget Henry as she drives like a maniac toward the interstate through fifteen miles of back country roads, saying to the windshield that Weldon's death will have one benefit. She ignores Weldon who is still alive, but so sick that he doesn't mind her talking about his death or her screaming "don't you die tonight, not tonight!" In fact, he had whispered to her when she pushed him into the front seat, dragging and half–carrying him from the house to the car, that he wanted to die.

To say the worst and either prevent it or get ready for it, Rebecca tells the rushing darkness of central Virginia about the benefit of Weldon's death, something they have both joked about and she has wondered about to various degrees over the years. If Weldon does die, Laura will of course stop her insistence that Rebecca come back to Weldon and the unhappy marriage. Look, she can say to Laura, I once did love, once deeply loved, completely loved this man. With Weldon dead, Laura may be at peace—even if it takes years. Now slumped against the door, he is breathing as if he were running away from the nausea that has made Rebecca stop three times for him to lean down out of the car to vomit. She held onto him to keep him from toppling out of the car. After the last time, she doesn't stop again.

They reach the interstate. Weldon's tux is wet with a glaze of saliva, all that's left in him to throw up.

Henry would go on talking, maybe claiming that he knows that there's nothing that Rebecca had not already thought about and said herself. He means murder. He might give a little soliloquy on murder, its history, the chances of indictment, of conviction. But no deer jump out at the car, no state trooper stops her for speeding—eighty-seven at her best—no tire goes flat, idiot lights on the dash stay dark, and finally, after the third exit, the gates to the hospital stand in front of the car.

The stiff neck, the nausea—Food poisoning? The beginning of another cluster of migraines? Weldon had eaten plates of lobster and shrimp at the wedding, washing them down with bourbon, dancing every dance, celebrating, he had said, not just for Laura but for himself and Rebecca the possibility of a double honeymoon. Father of the bride, husband of another bride, he said to the doctors who weren't listening.

"For real, go for it," one answered him, the Pakistani.

It was for real, she was going for it. Rebecca had come back home from the wedding with Weldon—they had walked straight down the brick walk of the Moorefields' home "Whitfield," right by Martha Travis who still looked hopeful in the rain, her pale silk dress ruined and her hair curling up tight against her neck. Evidently, Martha had driven to the wedding expecting to go home with Weldon in his car and stay over with him. That was their routine on other dates, one car left where ever they met. Laura has told Rebecca about the restaurants and the car retrievals after a night at home. Martha Travis's driving her car to meet Weldon was, according to Laura, a show of independence, coyness, even chastity, of indifference, and these were all strategies to interest Weldon. Then they would need to have a second date to go get her car from where it had been left the night before. Two cars, one bed, another date to retrieve her car.

Martha runs, Rebecca has heard from Laura, five miles a day, and looked at the wedding as if she might decide to whip out her running shoes and run alongside Weldon's car. Rebecca had driven to the wedding planning, like Martha Travis, to go home with Weldon. She knew that she could not resist Laura at her wedding, the weight of what she hoped for, the avalanche of yearning forcing Rebecca to be married to Weldon, at least for her wedding day. So Rebecca agreed in her heart that maybe it would not kill her—though they usually came close, these mini–reconciliations—to go home with Weldon and try, really try this time to stay where Laura and Weldon thought she belonged. Like Martha Travis, she knew an abandoned car was not a problem.

Gram has urged Rebecca to stay away, but then added that she could not insist because she loves Rebecca as much as she loves Weldon.

"I can tell you to come home just one more time," she

had said. "It takes all my strength, you know." She had laughed in a sweet co–conspiring way, in the spirit that had made it possible for Rebecca to stay away, on and off, over the ten years. If Gram had hated her, or hated Weldon, maybe the divorce would have gone through and been successful. Gram gave her permission to stay clear except on occasion when in lapses of judgment Rebecca let the past come back in full force making Weldon and her young again and their lives possible in movie flashbacks.

Rebecca's plan was for her car to wait for her in the Moorefield's field. It would spend the night there and then she and Weldon would come back for it the next day. The Martha Travis way, Rebecca thinks.

Liz McClellan is biding her time on the Weldon case. She is younger, forty-one, a modern, divorced woman with a nine year old boy at home, a big job with a credit card company, and is less invested in Weldon futures. And Weldon is not what he used to be, not what he once was, but there's a lot of good material there. "Many treasures still to be found on this <u>Titanic</u>," he likes to say. "Even the pyramids have some gold left in their cavities. A bracelet, a necklace maybe." Liz does not need to take expeditions for gold, though they are fun. She seems to be having fun being the old man's darling (Weldon is fifty–six) at public occasions when everyone will be thinking of Rebecca and lately of Martha when here is this new woman, this Liz.

Martha Travis, on the other hand, is the old–fashioned kind of woman (forty–seven) who will throw herself off a bridge or mix her lithium with vodka if things do not work out with Weldon. Rebecca, part of her, the part that Laura hated, did not want to stand in Ms. Travis' way with Weldon. But there he was, dancing his heart out with Liz

McClellan while Martha Travis disintegrated, knowing that in a few hours he was going home a (happily, he swore) married man.

Martha, so Rebecca has heard from Laura, has a Pacific Basin ABD from the University. The attraction is serious. It's not just her damp curls and runner's legs and his dark sadness and voice—perfect in their ways as matches. They are historians—they actually speak of themselves as 'historians'—and there is her natural, Nebraskan love of Weldon as a Virginian, Laura says, explaining that all states and especially the western ones love Virginia, a reverse manifest destiny, she says. Laura says that Martha sounds like a footnote when she talks. Things in the newspaper remind her of Dred Scott or Plessy v. Ferguson. Plus, more than her footnotes, she has the great appeal to Weldon of being on a perpetual job search, and this searching makes her seem young because of her anxiety and hope. She is not sure what direction to go in, she tells Laura who tells Rebecca. Not sure of a history position, she has managed to make a living as a herbalist/aerobics/hospice worker/dream interpreter/write–your–autobiography teacher, available for workshops and weekend retreats. Her latest area of skills is the Tellington–Touch method of getting to know a horse in order to improve self–esteem—both the rider's and the horse's. Martha knows, because Laura explains to her, that it is Rebecca and Weldon who are the true couple, the parents. Martha may love Weldon, but she must not, can not, will not be allowed to, marry him. Laura will listen and then crush Martha's hopes for her life, and it must be a mark of Weldon's old power, his charm, that she lets herself in for bashing by Laura.

Rebecca wavered before she left the Moorefield wedding scene. She decided that she would not stay all night in the sexual sense. It may be an all–night date, but there will be no sex for them on Laura's wedding night. A date does not have to mean anything sexual, especially if it is to try to begin married life again, that's all. Negotiation. She wanted it to be as different from her first date with Weldon as is possible, and different from what usually happens—a night of middle–aged sex followed by breakfast with Gram and sadness for two weeks.

Laura wanted the whole nine yards, renewed vows, marriage, party for friends, (would Martha Travis come?) parents at home, pre–grandparents. And that is what Rebecca herself would have loved to believe possible. Who doesn't want to be married, even in the late twentieth century! But those who are married, do they all want divorces or the kind of marriage Weldon has with dancing and dating historians in it?

On the drive to their honeymoon camping trip, Laura will be hoping that her parents went home together, expecting it, assuming it, seeing it happen. Wasn't that the whole idea that she had sold them on and that they all bought into? While Laura will be on her perfect honeymoon in the mountains, camping with her Jeremy Hill, her parents will be on their second honeymoon. Things will be balanced, well, except for Henry who seems to have accepted what he says is Laura's first marriage. Weldon is not serious about Martha Travis, Laura says. Martha T. is serious, but she has been warned, told what's what.

Rebecca's going home with Weldon, that idea, would be simply a wedding gift of the mother of the bride—herself, given in marriage by the daughter to her father. It is a gesture that Laura hopes with her whole heart will lead to a reinstatement, the reestablishment of the marriage, but of course, she understands that it may very well not. She knows that trains hit people, right, right, *right*.

But Laura knows that when Martha understands what comes with Weldon, Martha will be history. Gram comes with the package, as does the newly married Laura with Jeremy, the man who caused Henry's accident and then saved his life, and Jeremy is the least known of the little band; there is, of course, Henry with his worshipful parents heartbroken over his lost arm and his obsession with Laura. Then there is the competent Liz McClelland, trim and brown in her fuchsia linen with lime and navy trim, the new short style, plus her son who is at nine, already a national skeet shooting champion and soccer player; then add the Brightley tragedy, Kelly's death and all that it had meant for Weldon, Rebecca and Laura.

Rebecca saw no way out of Laura's dream for Weldon and her because of exactly what Laura has pointed out— history. Martha Travis should get out while the getting is good. She should shout, "I'm out of here." Rebecca wished she were Martha, a girl friend, not a wife. She'd have liked to be a ghost at the banquet, not the hostess or the caterer. A ghost, resting and floating, not the real–life woman who had dressed the meat, roasted it, poured the wine and then washed the dishes. So to speak.

It was crazy for her to think of staying with Weldon when he had Ms. Travis and then Ms. McClellan lined up, waiting for him to beckon. Laura's wish to have married parents should be shelved.

Rebecca feels that she can not be anyone's ideal mother,

and maybe not any kind of mother ever again if she lets Weldon die. Laura will never forgive Rebecca for Weldon's death on her wedding night. She may even have the death investigated and charge Rebecca with criminal neglect. Rebecca has heard of sisters taking out warrants against each other. Maybe children have parents arrested and charged. Laura will never forgive herself for trusting her father with her mother, and then she will commit suicide which will cause Henry to do the same, and Jeremy will work himself to death, having taken on six jobs to assuage his grief. Gram will live a few more weeks and then she will die. Rebecca will be left to serve her thirty year sentence. The stupidity of letting Laura's dream dictate Rebecca's life, not to mention the foolishness of it, is suffocating. Rebecca feels as if she has been shrink–wrapped and mailed to Weldon who, to show his gratitude for her going along with Laura's plan, is dying as she drives him to the hospital.

Death and destruction will come, are already here in spades, from trying to do what Laura wants in spite of experience, understanding, reading, counseling sessions, common sense and intuition. Renew broken and ruined wedding vows! Ones that show every sign of breaking immediately. Rebecca is angry to be pleased with herself for seeing so clearly what is bound to happen. Pleased to have driven so angrily (fast) without killing Weldon or without his dying before she got him to the hospital where he will certainly die. Angry that Weldon had a line of two women—Martha, Liz—waiting for him, three women, counting, as Laura would say, herself, his wife and mother of his only child: Rebecca.

Rebecca is not in any sense of the word jealous of

Martha Travis or Liz McClellan. There have been things too terrible in her life with Weldon (Kelly Brightley walks by across the fogged windshield, not Laura's age, but her own age when she died, just fourteen, pretty in her finch green stretch pants) for jealousy to be anything but a diversion, even a welcome one, a party favor at a wedding when everyone is dancing. Jealousy is something that can be gotten over or dealt with.

To Laura's credit at the wedding where she had a bride's privilege of saying anything to anyone, and where Rebecca fully expected Laura to campaign, to lecture, buttonhole, trap, Laura had not said one word. She had not gone into long explanations about her parents, about their marriage and why they should be together, not apart, should live happily, not waste their lives, should understand, not blame each other, on and on. Rebecca was sure that Laura did not speak to her on her favorite subject because she was so caught up in the work, the design of her own romance, the triangle she and Jeremy and Henry were engraving on everyone's memory. And because she expected this gift of compliance from her mother to be already wrapped and ready to deliver. The least her mother can do.

Martha Travis has confided in Laura who has explained to Rebecca and back to Martha that Martha Oliver Travis is not right for Weldon, nor he for her in spite of their mutual love of history and the Pacific Basin and in spite of her endeavors at choosing a career, finding a vocation, efforts that like the running are keeping Martha youthful, sinewy and with shiny, curling hair. One hundred seventeen pounds—Laura reports that Martha's weight has leveled off from a new juice and bean diet and helped her hair thicken that is a thousand shades of silver and brown.

Rebecca has weighed 143 since she was twelve, out of shape all of her life. "In every way," she thinks.

Laura has repeated Martha's meditations about her "relationship" with Weldon to Henry, to Rebecca, and probably to Jeremy, though he is the one least likely to listen, to tolerate hearing what this woman, Martha Travis, someone he does not want to know, he says, has in her head. Rebecca wishes she could be more like Jeremy: say what she will and won't listen to. This trait and his working three jobs as he goes to college are what she knows—not counting the train and Henry's arm—about Jeremy Hill.

Liz McClellan has not reached that level of confidential explanations from Laura yet, but her day is coming. Dancing and kissing socially are what Liz does in this phase of pursuing Weldon, and she also loves to talk to Weldon about her skeet–shooting son Nate, Laura says, but Martha Travis has reached the plateau of being mistaken about Weldon on every point, something Martha would probably agree with now after the wedding when standing alone in the rain, she watched him leave with Rebecca, his estranged wife, after she and Rebecca had watched him kiss Liz goodbye.

Laura had looked at Rebecca across the rose garden, across the dance floor, first from Jeremy's arms, then from Henry's one–armed embrace as if to say in formal, vatic, heraldic, hieratic diction: "Renew your vows for me, Mother, renew."

So after Laura and Jeremy left for their trip to the mountains—camping not just to save money but because they are experts at it—Weldon and Rebecca came back to what had been their home, the one where Gram has her little apartment which she calls her grotto on the side of the house, the one they had built of field stones picked up in a thousand twilights together, another piece of evidence of abiding love, a piece of history that Laura liked to toss around in her explanations.

They had not thought about the wedding seafood sitting out in chafing dishes on tables in the tents in the ninety degree evening. It never occurred to them that it was simply seafood that was what was wrong with Weldon, any more than it occurred to them that their strained efforts to do what Laura wanted them to do (be happy, be married) were killers. They were used to feeling off-center, not right, a sort of we–can't–go–on–we'll–go–on miasma that kept them from driving to the doctor until early the next morning. It was the wedding, the awkwardness of not being the hosts, of being guests at their daughter's wedding, of feeling too complicated to breathe much longer—all these things. Not *seafood* for God's sake.

Rebecca did not wake Gram up to tell her they are rushing off to the hospital—Gram is used to nocturnal troubles, leaving and arriving. She used to sleep through them, "hoping for safety, but knowing otherwise" she would say in pity and love for her son and Rebecca.

Weldon had been insisting, leaning toward Rebecca, across the cold, black slate table he had made for the kitchen, arguing as if she were objecting to what he was saying, that his life, such as it was, was his. He meant for her to understand that she was part of his life whether she admitted it or not, whether they divorced or not and whether they liked it or not. Martha Travis was a friend, yes, more than a friend, but not his wife, and not ever going to be unless Rebecca insisted on leaving him high and dry and going through with the unthinkable. He wanted what Laura wanted. His arms were hot against the chilled slate, and his hands when he reached for her were dry and heated.

Then his head touched down like a little plane flown by a person trying for a license but failing to impress the instructor strapped in the next seat, bumped down lightly a few times, just like a old box winged plane, then rested on the table, forehead to slate.

It should be easy for Rebecca to see why Laura goes along with Henry's plans for her, allowing Henry to call Jeremy Hill her first husband. She is used to grandiose plans that require human sacrifice. Having lived with Weldon, she has prepared herself, maybe without knowing it, for Henry. Laura is Henry's wife already, *period*, in spite of the wedding, in spite of Jeremy, the groom. Her marriage to Henry is a call waiting signal cutting through the present marriage, and though Henry will be a second husband, there is no doubt that he is the real husband. It should be easy for Rebecca to see what she is looking at.

Rebecca tried to say to Weldon that he is taking his usual amoral stand. That Laura is married to Jeremy Hill, *period*. She knows that Henry's certainty is as hard to resist as it is to accept.

"I am wrecked from trying to stay with or "date" you, Weldon, as you continue to kiss socially and dance as your own mother would have said, provocatively. Last year, I had shingles. This year, advanced anemia, both of which Laura thinks grow out of my deliberate and hateful ambivalence. Go home and be well, she tells me. Grow up. Take up your pallet, go home, and while you are at it, take iron."

Before Weldon's head dropped onto the table, he managed to say that Laura is used to living with plans that run counter to reality, but she knows that some angles are absolutely true, fitting tongue and groove into an ordinary, daily life. Of course she is. She has grown up with his plans to be happy with his wife, with Rebecca, regardless of what was actually happening. If there are problems deep rooted in personalities, then they must be ignored. If Rebecca has other plans, that is unfortunate.

Rebecca does feel guilty and unhappy about the situation, and has tried to be a part of the grand plan that Weldon and Laura have. Henry has diplomatically and momentarily stepped back from the situation, offering comments only when Laura gives him, as he says, a signed permission slip. Then he will say yes, he thinks that Rebecca might consider the beauty of tradition, that is, of acquiescence, and well, submission, (he is apologetic), necessary for women in order to have even a poor excuse for a marriage. He knows that statistically/emotionally marriage kills women and saves men, but he says those are the facts of the culture, not their faults, and because they cannot change the "true facts," they should try to live according to their best possibilities.

And so, Rebecca came home with Weldon from Laura's wedding intending to spend only part of the night, intending not to have the sex that both of them had thought of from the moment the band started playing "Who'll Stop the Rain" and "As Long as I Can See the Light" started, but instead she watched his head come to rest on the slate table. Then she drove him to the hospital and stayed with him until late the next afternoon, behind the curtained space in the emergency room at the hospital.

Standing over him and holding onto his shoulders as if she could at that late hour shake some sense into him. She would try if he would get well. He knew what she meant. They would be married if it killed them. Only later, let it be later that anyone was killed. Rebecca was crying those tearless tears that women in their forties cry, that Martha Travis knows about, that Liz McClellan probably does too.

Weldon was able to say up at her through dry lips that he had wanted them to die later and slowly, in a nursing home, not necessarily together, that was asking too much, but one after another, him first. Not suddenly and inconveniently like this and right after Laura's wedding, ruining her trip to the mountains. He wanted them to go to Henry's wedding and to dance in the rose garden again. He meant Laura and Henry's wedding. Rebecca saw that he was exhausting himself and made him shut up by saying shut up. He has always liked for her to say shut up because he grew up never hearing a woman say it. Being married to Rebecca has revealed a great deal to him, he has told her, about the twentieth century.

One of her many flaws is hating to be the bad guy.

"Come on, get hold of yourself. You don't have to look at things that way." He has heard her hundreds of times go on about getting hold, and looking at the world a different way.

This time she meant the same thing, only more.

Young men, just a little older than Laura, brought Rebecca reports from the spinal tap. Higher levels of white cells. Elevations, concern, another tap. Still, they had hope for the antibiotics dripping rapidly into Weldon, who turned, or tried to, straining slightly against her grip on his shoulders, on the hard plastic gurney and gave her a look, as if she were his boat at Cobbs Creek and he was swimming for it in a slow breast stroke, reaching for the rope ladder then reconsidering and waving it away, trying to, only she caught hold of his shoulders and made him hold on. He meant to strike off to some island she could not see, perhaps send Martha Travis a note in a bottle or send up smoke signals to Liz McClellan.

Oh yes, now that Rebecca has just renewed her vows to Weldon on his death bed, he wants to strike out for open water, the ocean, to leave her again, letting her think he had no choice, that there was an implied obligation on her part to Martha or Liz. Outrageous, but life confirming. The old and true Weldon. She could hear him say almost:

"You and Laura go on without me, I'll keep swimming out here for a while."

That's exactly Weldon. One slight advantage—in this case a sentence commuted—and he's back to his old ways.

CHAPTER THREE

The Moorefield house was still full of the flowers when Rebecca drove the forty–three miles over there at dusk, having settled Weldon with Gram. Weldon was weak but out of the woods. She wanted to ask the Moorefields if she could help with the aftermath of the wedding and if it would be all right for her to leave her car there for a day or two.

Vivian Moorefield told her that Henry wanted the flowers left until Laura got back. Then he would return to dry them for arrangements. Most young men in America do not dry flowers for arrangements, even young men studying mortuary science. Some of the cut roses had been dripping petals at the wedding. The caterers had cleaned up everything else. The old house, except for the flowers still in the big hanging baskets in the oak trees and the trampled grass, looked as if nothing had happened; just yesterday there had been two hundred and thirty–seven people there, James Moorefield had said. He'd counted them as he stood at the window.

So there is Henry's mother in the yard dropping aspirin in the huge vases and carrying a cutting board and bread knife around to each vase and basket so that she can slice the stems off diagonally and give the flowers a few more days. Rebecca does not tell her about Weldon's sudden illness—it's over, he's home, no one died and it is clear that Vivian Moorefield would not be too sorry if one or more of Laura's untidy family would die suddenly. And because it has turned out to be something set off by the seafood--not salmonella exactly, but some allergic reaction--Rebecca does not say anything. The Moorefields had paid for the seafood and everything else, and no one else as far as Rebecca knows has gotten sick, not that she has the Moorefields' phone number.

Rebecca carries the stepladder for Vivian to climb up to the baskets of flowers beaten down by the rain but still themselves, roses, lilies, ivies, to drop the aspirin in or to snip the stems.

In the Moorefields' house, the phone is ringing as they move toward the open front door. The machine takes the call. Laura's voice is asking for Henry. Because Rebecca knows Laura and Henry and Jeremy better than Vivian does—at least she thinks does—she is not surprised, but she can see Vivian's mother's neck go tight and her elbow tremble. "Where did Laura and Jeremy go on their wedding trip?" She does not use "honeymoon."

"To the mountains."

That's the end of the conversation. Then they are back to giving the flowers aspirin and cutting their stems.

In the garden, Laura had stood by the rose called Brandy and smoked a cigarette, beautiful in her long dress and relieved expression. She had started smoking again. Henry, of course, announced that Laura had convinced him, so he lit up as if he had been smoking all his life, using the gangster, straight–down from his nether lip technique.

At last, Laura's long arms in white said. At last, her grandmother's amethyst pendant said. At last, Rebecca felt herself saying.

No one thought Laura and Jeremy would make it, would marry—they fought too much. During their phone calls, Laura would furiously explain why Jeremy had been wrong, how he did not understand the way she was thinking or what she was doing. Every time she hung up, it seemed that she did not say goodbye. Mid–sentence clicks or slams.

As far as Rebecca knows, the train had been the deciding reason for the marriage. The Henry factor might seem a problem but as Laura explained, it was not. Laura wanted to set an example to follow. If her parents would not follow her advice, her tens of thousands of words, the long hours of tearful explanations about their lives and their necessities, then she would show them: marry an impossible person, impossible for her anyway and make a success of it. Jeremy Hill would offer living proof of the possibility of making the wrong person the right husband. She would marry in the full knowledge that someone else loved her and yes, she deeply loved Jeremy. And Henry. Marriage was marriage; love was love. Had her parents never heard that romantic love was a recent invention, like the electric light bulb or e–mail.

Laura's sympathies were and are entirely with Weldon. He has suffered, his life has been blighted. Rebecca is the one who does not understand true love and certainly not marriage. She is the one who has the problem. Weldon was, Laura would admit, the wrong person for Rebecca, but Rebecca is the one who must make the marriage go forward. Unfair, but there it is.

And so, next to the roses banked in new perfectly rounded mulch, Laura had married Jeremy. Weldon had stood by Rebecca, and Weldon and Rebecca Cauthorn were for those few hours at the wedding, dancing and eating lobster in the heat, talking and laughing, a conversation piece, publicly married for the afternoon after the ten years of being separated. Rebecca felt the interest in them shoot little flames out of their shoulder blades—even next to the bride, groom and best man she and Weldon are interesting. Martha and Liz are their bridesmaids.

Rebecca's great–grandfather's favorite book had been *Napoleon and His Marshalls*, and the opening line has been handed down to her: "It is the greatest misfortune for a man to be born next to a great man." Laura meant her marriage to be her parents' good fortune; it would help them to see an ideal. If it sounds crazy, well, it was.

At the wedding, next to the triangle Jeremy–Laura–Henry, Rebecca and Weldon held their own. Understanding it differently, they try to be the best they can be. The beauty of the bride and groom, their youth, their absolute trust in themselves to overcome difficulties with each other was already apparent, blinding even, and Rebecca and Weldon shaded their eyes, united in this view completely, and danced on, trying to be married for Laura's sake.

Everywhere on the Moorefield's lawn in the light rain, people wanted to be near them, not to talk to them, but to look at them, to see what was going on. Rebecca and Weldon. They don't understand why they put up with each other; *get a life* each of them has been told. Middle–aged teenagers.

Weldon's secret is that he does not want a different life. He likes his life as is, and Rebecca does not know how to get another one, how to change her life or Weldon's under the scrutiny of their daughter whom they have worshipped instead of loved, a deadly reversal, according to another family piece of wisdom.

The Moorefields, Vivian and James, always tried not to be interested in the Cauthorns and were relieved that Laura decided to marry Jeremy, not Henry, even if they had to give her the wedding. They were, even so, sick at heart because it must have been apparent to them that their Henry was still obsessed with Laura and nothing they saw or heard—the little information about the Cauthorns that they allowed into their "cognitive maps" as Henry said—could dispel the "utter gloom" (again, Henry's description of their response to his troubles and also to the fact that they were hosting a wedding for the young woman who would not marry, and *thank God* for that, their Henry).

What did Jeremy Hill think of this situation? Laura explained, probably even to the resistant Moorefields, that Jeremy did not handle explanations well at all. He, it seems, lived, acted and had his being beyond words.

So, why did the Moorefields offer their home for Laura and Jeremy's wedding? Simple. They had no choice. Henry wanted the wedding there. Henry has said that his parents always expect complications, that this expectation is their most lovable trait as parents and makes up for their other "lacunae" such as never attending any of his school events, even his forensics matches at the state level, much less his soccer tournaments when he had two arms.

Further, Henry says, his parents have their own romance, adding stalely and drolly, that all parents claim one, but his really do have dibs on one: old money lost, new money made (in lumber and landfills) and almost lost again, plus his mother was an orphan bride. Hard to beat, he has told Rebecca. That outline is what she knows, *in toto*, about the Moorefields.

At the wedding, James Moorefield went back into the house after the ten minute service, while Vivian Moorefield floated wearily outdoors, worrying about drinks (but not the seafood in the warm September dusk) and pointing out roses blooming so late, just right for the wedding. Cornering anyone who smiled at her with a little garden club lecture on roses. They existed thirty–five to forty million years ago. Many believe the rose was the first flower grown for a garden. Not a cabbage as some claim. Here she will turn slightly away from the cornered guest but goes on about rose leaf fossils found in Montana and Oregon.

She will explain that "old roses" bloom once a year, in early summer. Hers did. Her moss and damask, the yellow brier, the Tudor. The hybrid perpetuals are the ones that are making the wedding so... she hesitates and does not need to finish. The first tea rose, that one over there, she points, was developed in 1867. "Spice Twice" it's called according to her friend at the Rose Center, Reid Douglass. By now the guest has tapped on his empty glass and apologized for dying for a refill and eased himself out of her range.

Henry has said Vivian—he calls her Vivian—has a deflective way of talking, glancing, oblique. It works. Provides context and packing, dry Styrofoam peanuts, layers of bubbled plastic, which she put around the afternoon.

Rebecca gets caught up in the miracle of the late roses Vivian points out, and if she does not forget the tragedy of the wedding, she lives through it.

"Do come in for something, at least a glass of tea. I can't let you drive home without something after your help with the flowers."

Rebecca looks at Vivian, her hands full of dead flowers and scissors, the aspirin bottle stuck in her belt. Her hair is faintly red, a pinkish gray, and cut as short as an astronaut's. Her eyes are as wild as Rebecca's. Neither has been to bed since the day before the wedding which is now almost exactly twenty–four hours over. Forty–six hours of being on their feet. Dangerous women, wary, circling, but they go in the house where Henry's father is standing by the long window that he had stood by yesterday.

James Moorefield looks at Rebecca the way he would look at a prowler—shocked but knowing the gun is near at hand. He says "Hello, Mrs. Cauthorn."

Rebecca has on the suit she wore to the wedding, which he stares at, the wrinkles and water streaks where she wiped off Weldon's vomit in the hospital bathroom.

"Like Mrs. Kennedy," he says in a thoughtful way. Is this a terrible thing to say or something it took courage to say? Three words from this man is a long–winded speech, and so far, there have been six. "Your car is out in the field from yesterday." Then he turns away. Fifteen words so far.

Vivian washes the glass she gets out of the cabinet and then polishes it with a flimsy tea towel. Why is she washing a clean glass? Then she cracks ice in the towel the way Rebecca's mother used to, wrapping a few cubes in the towel and hitting them with the handle of a knife as she holds the little sack of tea towel and ice in the palm of her hand. She uses a silver knife and dents it with each hit. The iced tea is delicious in the shales of ice. Hand–cracked ice!

"I should tell you, I think, if Henry has not already, that my father's younger brother, Lawrence, was shot when he was only twenty–three. He loved someone else's bride.

He built a house on a hill that looked down on the young married couple, had it ready to live in, camp out in by the time they were back from their wedding trip. It was a six-week honeymoon, so he had those weeks to throw up his house, got in a crew of men and framed it and roofed it, had it standing when they returned. The young husband shot him early one morning but was never charged with murder. They still live there and Lawrence's house is used for a hay barn. The couple bought the few acres Lawrence had and nothing was ever said. Henry knows this story about his murdered uncle. I am afraid that it appeals to him.

"This is one of the reasons I am worried so about Henry who will be twenty-one soon. Excuse me for talking so much. I am embarrassing James, but he feels the same way. I wish things worked out for young people, but of course, they don't, and now your Laura is married to Jeremy, who seems to be--who is, I am sure--a very fine young man, different from Henry, but in his own way, very fine, don't you agree? My other young uncle shot himself when he was twenty-three. In my family, youth can be difficult, especially for the men. Most of the young men, all of them in my generation, did not make it through youth, we always say. Henry is the last one of my family, and James has one cousin."

Rebecca asks about the young uncle who was killed by the jealous husband. Had Lawrence come for a visit, had he appeared suddenly? Henry has never told her that story.

"The most amazing thing is this, though. When the murderer, the young husband, a few years later was dying—bone cancer—my father went to him and sat down at his table which was beside the bed, and ate with him, or as we always said, broke bread with him, and forgave him. Then he died, the murderer died. My father came on back home and told us about it, how the young wife—we always thought of them as the bride and groom or the young wife and husband—poured Daddy coffee and offered him a slice of pie. He could not get over being offered pie in such circumstances, though nothing would have worked or made any more sense than pie, he used to say."

Rebecca drinks the perfectly made tea. Steeped in a Japanese pot, still warm with the ice cracking like small pistols in the huge glass, a leg of mint standing in it top to bottom. She asks for sugar and puts in three tablespoons.

The answering machine is winking a red light. Rebecca looks at it hoping that Vivian or James will repeat the message that must be the one they heard from Laura as they were working on the flowers. Rebecca is glad they have not deleted it.

Vivian is looking in her refrigerator and finds a dish. It is the seafood only it's in a cut glass bowl now, much smaller than the wide trencher of a server used by the caterers at the wedding. Under the fogged Saran Wrap, it's a delicate pink, safe. Vivian is fixing a plate for Weldon for Rebecca to carry home.

Rebecca does not know how much Vivian knows about her, where she is living and trying to live in two different places, and where she will come back for her car from. She thinks that she must know everything from Henry, but then, Vivian seems surprised that Rebecca does not know about her murdered Uncle Lawrence or the other one who shot himself.

Rebecca is drawn to the young Uncle Lawrence. The suicide uncle can wait. That could be anything, but a murdered young uncle worries her. She can ask about him. Isn't it Vivian who started this conversation, launching off into the deep ocean as soon as she fixed the tea? Maybe she expects an exchange of stories about family murders.

"And, what exactly did your uncle do to be murdered? Building a house on a hill, was it a threat? I can see that it might have been seen as one by the young husband, but wasn't it legal?" Rebecca shakes her tea in the slivered ice. It has a wonderful slurred taste, sweet and with jets of mint.

"We are not sure what Lawrence did. James says it must have had to do with the young wife, he must have spoken to her in a way that made the young husband go in the house for his gun. Not too long ago, you could be shot for even looking at another man's wife. James thinks that more than looking was going on. Maybe the young wife returned the look. Young women do, sometimes, some of them, invite attention, especially praise. I know one young woman, your daughter, Laura, who tells the truth about this: never enough, she has said to me, never, never enough praise. She is remarkable to say that, don't you think? No one, I have said to James, even in Virginia, kills a man for looking at a married woman, but your Uncle Lawrence ended up murdered, James says to me. I never knew Uncle Lawrence, but I grew up hearing about him and about my father going to visit the murderer when he called him to sit with him as he was dying—so they must have been friends at least. Never charged, never served a day, but soon dead with bone cancer."

All Rebecca's questions seem answered, so she begins to get up. Vivian has the bowl ready and has put it in a cooler with ice so there "is no danger" from the heat. She runs her hands through her short hair and starts talking as if

Rebecca has asked her about why her hair is so short.

"Don't laugh at me when I tell you that I thought I could get Henry's attention by almost shaving my head. Maybe he would even think I had gone for chemo. I was looking for a way to shock him, but as you know, he thinks he has experienced the ultimate shock—not the arm, *just an arm,* he says, and I know that you have heard him say, brag almost, that he has another one. The wedding--that's what shocked him and that's why we agreed to have the wedding here. To help Henry, I mean to try to help him, to let him see that Laura had chosen someone else to marry. We thought maybe if he saw her married here, saw us going along with it, that he would, as he would say, be more *sanguine.* More accepting of the inevitable. Whatever, as he would say. So, in July, with the wedding two months away, I walked into a barber shop, the old-fashioned kind for men, and forced the poor man to cut my hair. It was long, has been since I was a girl. He cut and cut. He said I was making him cry, and I said good, I hoped my son would. James thought it was a good idea when I got home and explained what I was doing. My head still feels light, and no, it did not make Henry think of chemo or of a long, terminal illness and the necessity of his growing up. Now I like my hair short and have been back again to that barber shop." Vivian pauses. "I hope I haven't talked too much and frightened you. James says I must give myself out in small doses, as I have such deep waters to draw from. James can make terrible things seem like gifts—Henry, as you know, is like that too—only I am afraid for him, well, for both of our children, yours and ours."

Things are clearer but worse to Rebecca, and she feels that she must leave, not drink more tea, not ask any questions, not understand any more than she does at this point. Vivian and James walk her out to the car where she left it, far away in the field, parked down near the barn to start a row of cars for the crowd that was here yesterday.

Rebecca walks in the middle, Vivian carries the bowl of seafood salad, James holds her elbow and helps her into the car, shutting it with a careful and firm push, then he pushes down the lock.

Through the window, safe beyond the locked door, he urges her to come back to see them. "Bring your husband," he says and adds, "I didn't have a chance to talk to him yesterday."

Chapter Four

Weldon and Rebecca, like the married couple they are trying to turn into, sit again at the kitchen table four days after Laura's wedding. They look and feel like hell, but are doing their best. Everything supports their charade: hospital event safely under their belts, daughter married and honeymooning, an extra person in love with their daughter, all going nicely.

They look out of the windows that are ground level and go up to the ceiling. These windows are, in fact, glass doors they had found in an old house that was being torn down; so all of the windows in their stone house, even on the second floor, are old doors. Some open and have screens. They put them in the last summer Rebecca lived at home. Everything in this house marks a time when she was coming back or leaving: There's the tree house shingled with tin cans; there's the canoe for the river, the gazebo, the gravel walk through yuccas and azaleas, the lily pond, the brattle work; there's the English mastiff, Duchess.

Rebecca and Weldon stare out of the windows confident for this moment in their house, poised in this moment as marrieds who still have a seventy thousand dollar mortgage together—they split the payments, whether they were living together or not, over the years ever hopeful that these accumulated facts about their lives will combine to somehow bring them luck so that they will become what they are either pretending or trying to be: married. These windows might still bring them what they had once thought they would bring when they unloaded them one by one, stacking them criss–crossed on pallets and covering them with a plastic tarp—the one Laura and Jeremy took to put under their honeymoon tent.

It's three–thirty. They are totting up hours to show Laura, dropping pennies in the old stone crock until it's too heavy to lift and has to be unloaded into penny sleeves from the bank, oh yes, building up their investment in time spent married, for Laura. Spending is the metaphor Laura has often used to show her parents why they have too much to lose if they do not resume their marriage—read her lips, "Rebecca must not leave again. There are time shares in this condominium of married life, look, they've paid for them, they should take advantage."

And it *is* the fourth day after the wedding. *Tempus fugit*, not to brag. Tuesday, September eighteenth. Though there is a slight, unpleasant note of effort, a cello's thrum saying this is serious, that makes them careful not to feel like hostages marking off days or organ transplant survivors proud of each hour's march toward recovery.

One of the time–management–marital-strategies which Laura has given them is "committing to small projects," as ways to build toward the impossible ones like staying married or building a stone house with field stones picked up, not trucked in from a quarry, and windows made from salvaged doors. So, like the good parents they want to be, they are planning a small project: later they will drive over to the Moorefields' to get Rebecca's car. They do not have to go into what this small plan means to their marriage, but the plan does make them feel on top of things. Laura is right about small plans. So maybe, who knows, she is right about big ones. They are happy to be pleasing her.

They do not mention any of their left–over problems—

Martha Travis or Liz McClanahan—or ongoing realities—Kelly Brightley's death, their debts, their *residual anger* as one counselor called it.

They can handle the car problem, drive over to New Kent County together, speak to the Moorefields if they want to speak, return the cut glass bowl (Rebecca threw the seafood away on her drive home) and hope that they do not see them for the next three or four centuries at least.

Rebecca has told Weldon about Henry's murdered great–uncle and the one who killed himself. He likes the stories as she was afraid he would.

The air conditioning makes steam on the tall windows. The trees are not showing the first sign of red or yellow, the rain has turned the woods into the tropics, and the green leaves shine green lights into the late afternoon. Someone is walking down the road, a strange sight, "weird" as Laura would say, because no one walks in the country now even to their mailboxes, except for the few retired people who exercise as if they still lived in the city, wearing earphones, and walking in fast, purposeful ways, using every muscle possible to the musical instructions in their ears. Young people run, the athletes already into football season since the first of August, running the six mile loop by the Cauthorn place and the river, but they run early in the morning. Laura can do a mile she says in "under six, easy, and when I try, under five." This figure out of the windows does not move in walking, jerking, aerobic ways. Certainly, it is not a football runner coming toward them as they sit, married, behind their steamed windows, but a shape that hangs in the green dusk, walking, walking, as if the camera had slowed down and the walker is caught in the lens coming toward the waiting, not knowing viewers.

And, all at once, it is Laura, leaning against the air, falling forward toward them in little three–step runs, zig-zagging toward them; Rebecca and Weldon are up, lunging toward her, the slate table in their way, in each other's way, bruising themselves as they fight to get around the table and open the door, across the porch and down the yard slope, down into the road.

Then they are with Laura and back already at the porch. She is sagging against Weldon who has gotten himself to her first, and by himself gotten her back to the door. This is happening still in slow motion, but also instantly, so quickly that Henry's dead uncles are left in the room from Rebecca's report to Weldon and they watch what's happening.

The returned bride looks as if she has been attacked in a parking lot, kidnapped and then dropped off on a country road, beaten, maybe raped, but not killed. Not killed, no, still alive.

Recently a pick–up truck prowling around a three–county area has been signaling lone women drivers to pull over because there is something wrong with their cars, and the driver motions to them looking in their rear view mirrors back at him, helpfully pointing to the shoulder of the road. Something must be dragging, something loose from the engine, something which he has seen driving behind them. The women stop, and he asks them to get out of their cars and look at what he has seen. Then he rapes them, then kills them, then throws them out on a deserted road or in a pond. Three women so far in the past year.

Laura is walking, or trying to with Weldon's help, across the porch. Rebecca and Weldon are thinking of the man in the white pick–up as Laura slips through Weldon's arms, bloodied and dirty. Laura would have outsmarted him, gotten out of her car (What car? She was on her honeymoon, not driving country roads alone) with a tire iron, with her twenty–two, with a broken beer bottle and taken him down before he got into his psychopathic fixation–getalong.

Laura has rescued herself from the white–pickup murderer! But there have been four rapes in the county in the last five years, and one was maybe not a rape exactly because Donna Medrick told the Commonwealth's Attorney that she enjoyed it in some ways, though she reported it, and she seemed to enjoy all the questions too.

Laura is not the bride come home joyous, blooming, filled with love, from a camping trip with her new husband, the Hit–me Train, the iron man, the offensive–defensive–both–ways scholarship groom, coaches' award winner, first–team all–district man whose camping gear Rebecca and Weldon have heard catalogued: The stove, the three–hundred dollar sleeping bags, the tent, the binoculars and camera, the boots.

"Jeremy blew up the car."

Laura is sinking down again through Weldon's arms onto the floor. He is getting a new grip under her knees and clamping her shoulders, lifting her up, still in the reflex of welcoming her, as the gesture turns into emergency action. He bends and lets her feet brush the porch floor, trying to make her stand up on her own or see if she can. She must try. Then, he is carrying her into the living room and putting her on the sofa as Rebecca follows.

Dried blood runs in zippers cross her face.

"Jeremy blew up the car."

Then she shudders and tries to vomit, only she can't sit

up. Weldon helps her, holds her head as he used to when she was a child, and Rebecca runs to the phone as Weldon is saying, "Call Henry at his mother's."

But Rebecca calls the hospital and says the ambulance is coming.

A new world is taking shape as the fifth day after the wedding passes, back at home from the hospital again, for the second time after the wedding, this time with Laura. They are parents home with their baby—twenty–two years later.

At last Laura has them where she wants them, her parents are at home, together. This is a story for an inspirational article in *The Reader's Digest*: Parents reconcile in order to care for their injured daughter whose last request from her death bed (better not mention honeymoon) is for her parents' reunion.

Rebecca feels that she is dying, and that the only cure will be Laura's explanation. She craves knowing what has happened in the mountains? Why did Jeremy blow up the car—and how did he do it, and do it without killing both of them? Why isn't he with Laura? Is he in a hospital somewhere? Do his parents know? Why haven't the Hills called them? For that matter, why don't they rush to the phone to call the Hills? What would they say? Jeremy blew up his car? Your son could have killed our daughter? Laura is almost dead and Jeremy may be dead? Why is Laura here alone? How did she get here?

This bride of brides who planned every minute of her wedding, her life and her parents' life!

And now Henry is here, moved in, it seems. He will

be sleeping on the floor in a sleeping bag, so that he can jump up if Laura needs him; and Gram, of course, is here, but as she says, "barely here, glad to be of use, but not able to be much use." She is quiet, and her companion Ruby Witt (who is only a few years younger than Gram, her friend from the third grade, who "left school in the sixth, while her friend Gram "went on to be a school teacher,") is almost living here, going home late at night if she goes at all. Ruby moved in when Rebecca left the last time and is not surprised that Rebecca is back.

"Can't surprise me," Ruby brags. Gram will add when she is up to it, "But, you can me. We are a perfect pair."

Things are so terrible that Rebecca thinks why not call Martha Travis and Liz McClellan. Why not? The wrong people are here, so why not ask some more wrong people. She corrects herself. Maybe they are the right people here only at the wrong time.

Rebecca tells herself exactly who is at home with her and Weldon. Beginning the roll, counting as if for a class or a party, talking to herself: Weldon, the old almost-ex–husband is here, but Jeremy, the new groom is absent.

A blended family, Henry starts calling them, measuring out upbeat doses depending on how much cheer he thinks they can take from his own overflowing happiness, if it is happiness that is stirred in with great anxiety about Laura who has not moved since Weldon put her in bed when they got home from the hospital.

Rebecca has to keep naming them, telling herself who is here and how they got here. She calls the roll: she is Rebecca, she says for her own benefit like a woman in a magazine who is introducing herself, getting ready to have herself made over, give herself over to cosmetic and hair experts: "I am forty–three, I have been, for the ten years before my daughter's wedding, more or less separated from my husband, the one I had been 'dating,' 'seeing,' and having occasional sex with, which we said was for our daughter's sake. Since the wedding four days ago, I think it was four, maybe five, I have been reunited, remarried. There is Weldon himself, his mother, and her companion–friend, Ruby Witt, and now, the bride, our daughter, Laura Addison Cauthorn Hill is here. Henry Moorefield, the best man, is here and seems to be planning to live here. The groom, I keep saying, is not here, and so far, he has not been mentioned except in these five words, 'Jeremy blew up the car.'"

Rebecca falls into silence, praying for Laura to tell them what has happened. And as they wait, Rebecca continues an argument with Laura in her head as if Laura could hear her, as if she were sitting up drinking her Earl Grey, listening to her mother, as if Rebecca Cauthorn were the interesting one; Rebecca goes on justifying her life, telling the stories of her separations from Weldon, trying to make Laura see Weldon the way she does, pretending that Laura is sitting up in her bridal bed, that Jeremy is down the hall brushing his teeth or cleaning the stove from the camping trip. It is an exercise in futility, foolishness, one–sided, a monologue, hogging the conversation, neurotic, motherly.

On the other hand, she is trying to make Laura interested in them again, so that she will sit up and explain why she is there at home in her bed, turned to the wall, the one movement she has made since Weldon carried her down the hall to her old room, home from the hospital, the room still filled with gift wrap and tissue paper that she was using for the bridesmaids' presents: Three pewter Jefferson cups from the Monticello gift shop, engraved, twenty–nine ninety–seven, charged on Rebecca's Visa card.

Weldon's two hospital visits are showing on him. His hands shake as he builds a fire in Laura's bedroom in the miniature Swedish stove they put in there before the room had a chimney; back–assed, Weldon called it, getting the stove, then building the chimney. Tomorrow by mid-morning the sun will have warmed the house, but he does not want Laura to feel the dampness the rains brought. They must not beteem her face, he would say if he were talking. He will bring her the coffee she has loved since she was three years old, brewed with egg shells as the filter, tomorrow. No more of this silly tea–drinking, picked up in college.

Laura shivers under the quilt even after the fire is going, the air conditioning off, the windows open to let in the September heat. She does not know that Rebecca has not always tried to leave Weldon. Rebecca hopes that her stories, her monologues will catch Laura's attention, hook it and pull her back into her life. Laura thinks that Rebecca has spent all of her energy resisting Weldon, his great appeal, diluting it, denying it, undermining it, deflecting it. The secret fact is that for the first decade of their lives together, Rebecca tried to keep Weldon from leaving home, wanted him to have his flings, enjoy himself, keep sowing his wild oats, but come home, *just come home*, just so they stayed married. She was a Laura for ten years—*stay married*, her mantra—until Laura was ten, then Rebecca began leaving in her own fashion, that is, leaving and returning. Then when Laura was fifteen, Rebecca left for good, well almost, more or less.

Once Rebecca threw her wedding ring—it was Weldon's

grandmother's—into the river as they were driving across the bridge, once she locked him in the house, once she shot the gun in the air not knowing which one of them she wished would catch the falling bullet, and one year she tried to run away with his friend Tom Clary. These were all attempts to save the marriage, either to keep Weldon at home or to make it possible for her to stay at home. The stories that could come from these events should lure Laura out of her bed, out of her trance, wake her up. When has she ever been able to resist explaining her parents?

Laura knows the surface of these stories. She has certainly lived through them, watching from her room with the Swedish stove in it. To her, they have all boiled down to one miserable truth: Weldon was driven away from home, leaving in despair at Rebecca's "negative" and "unimaginative way of looking at the world." The way Rebecca calls the true way. Nothing worked to keep Weldon at home, to keep him married, except separation— listen closely, Laura, Rebecca wants to say, but just shifts the tone of her voice.

"Once your mother, believe it or not, Laura, left for good. Five years ago—that's when your father, your beloved father, wanted to be married, stay at home. Any teenager could have told me that. You could have. Hard–to–get is most loved. I thought pitching the old ring in the river would make Weldon a true and faithful husband, or locking the doors or shooting into the air would help. Fairy tale remedies, every one: the golden ring tumbles down into the dark currents of the river where an ancient carp noses it and swallows it for centuries. Locked in the stone house, the husband grows old and wise; animals come to the windows and bring him herbs and flowers. The bullet lodges next to the husband's heart, cauterizing it and healing him of all past wrongs and pain. You can see how I was thinking, Laura."

Rebecca hopes against hope that Laura will say, as she has on any other matter but this one of Weldon's being wrong, of his needing to be healed, "Yeah, right."

"Actually," which is another one of Laura's favorite words, when Rebecca locked the door, Weldon walked out another door; there was only one lock on the stone house with twelve window/doors. When she shot the gun the bullet hit an oak tree and shook down a bundle of mistletoe which made him laugh and bring it to her before he left, and when she went out with Tom Clary, Weldon followed them pulling up into the parking lots of the restaurants, acting as if he had invited them out to dinner with him. He picked up the checks. Tom said he couldn't go on with her if Weldon paid for the date. It was *sick*, too much for him.

Then, five years ago, Rebecca moved out. Just as Ann Landers or any girl in America says will happen, Weldon started getting serious about wanting to be married. People around here said they were wasting each other's time, not to mention theirs, throwing their lives away on each other, acting like fools, teenagers, idiots. They should get divorced as everyone else does in the twentieth century. When Rebecca told Weldon that Ruby Witt had told her what people were saying, Weldon asked who else should be throwing their lives away.

Laura has deep scratches on her face, but nothing is broken, the same doctors, the very ones who had seen Weldon after the seafood poisoning from the wedding, said at the emergency room.

These same doctors took Rebecca and Weldon into an office—Henry was not invited in because they did not understand who he was or why he was there, and Rebecca did not explain, just said no, he was not Laura's brother or husband. The young doctors said there was not much they could do at the hospital and that Laura might as well be at home.

The pregnancy was one they considered extremely risky because of her obvious state of exhaustion and her responses to them. They assumed that Rebecca and Weldon knew about it, and in fact, they have begun to feel that they have always known it now that they do know it. Not that it explains anything.

Henry had met them at the hospital, his clothes thrown in a garbage bag in the back of the Thunderbird. For the first time in Rebecca's experience, he was silent—for him. "Thank you for calling me," he had said. "Of course, I'll be moving in with you," and hung up. He was there in twenty–seven minutes.

"Fifty–seven miles in twenty–seven," he apologized.

Thinking about it, Rebecca is sure that Laura had been calling Henry and that she had heard the message when she was at the Moorefields' the day after the wedding—what, four, five days ago now? Four, five centuries ago?

She and Weldon now have this new thing in common: aging rapidly, a hundred years per day. Laura may feel some hope from their ancient looks about their future as a couple if she ever begins her old crusade again of getting her parents to stay married, to be married, to act married at the very least. And now of course, they wish that she would, that she could rise to the old occasion. Now they will stay married regardless. That part of life is over. Maybe they have grown up. So, they are at home, Weldon and Rebecca, married again forever, happy, unhappy, to hell with it.

They will get up with a baby born prematurely, as the doctors predict will happen if they are not careful. Who else is there to take Laura to the hospital when the baby is born or to the doctors for the check–ups? Who else is there to try to find Jeremy? Rebecca does not think of Henry though he is there and has spread out his books around his sleeping bag in the hall that runs by Laura's room.

Sometime in the first forty–eight hours of the honeymoon, Jeremy vanished, after he "blew up the car," leaving Laura to walk, to hitchhike home from Old Rag Mountain. Madison County, it's at least sixty miles away. She did not call them. Evidently, she called Henry to tell him. There was no message for them on Weldon's phone when they got home from the hospital the night/morning after the wedding. Rebecca is guessing at all of these things. Laura called Henry at his parents, but he was not there when Rebecca was helping with the flowers. When he got the message, he was paralyzed. Laura did not leave a number—her phone did not give it for some reason—or any detail to help him find her so he stayed by the phone waiting. The next call was from Weldon at the hospital with Laura.

The next morning, now the sixth day, Henry talks to Laura, to the back of her head, to her closed eyes. He tells her that the call to him from her honeymoon makes him happy, just to think about it. It saved his life he tells her, not many rival suitors get a call from the bride of thirty–six hours into marital bliss. He had been planning an unassisted suicide when the call came, when he dropped by his parents to pick up the suit he wanted to be buried in. Rebecca and Weldon hear and see him trying all of his tricks: comedy, tragedy, stand–up comedy, songs, poems, all that he knows. He even reads her a paragraph from her sixth grade geography book—on rivers. He says all the poems he knows and makes up new endings for them.

And then, he is saying, retelling his suicide preparation story again. A miracle! His Laura calls him and then, better still, she simply shows up four days or is it five after her wedding! It shows, he dances around the foot of her bed and taps on her stove warm with its little fire rattling in it, that they live in an age of miracles. He is on alert, in attendance. Ready to take arms against this sea of trouble. Then he adds, "And by opposing, end them."

Laura does not move, except to shiver. She is not in a coma, she is not asleep, but she is not awake. Henry cannot shut up. He tells Rebecca and Weldon in a high, Rocky Mountain mania, that he hopes, he prays, that this baby is his—it is clear that he thinks of the baby as his Baby Girl, for the moment and forever, and regardless of this sad honeymoon experience, he says that she is, anyway, half Laura Cauthorn's (not Laura Hill's), so who cares about the other half of the baby? All due respect to present company, he says, parentage—biological—is not a big deal. Jeremy Hill was his best friend until—here he hesitates, worried, he says about what the unborn baby should know at this point—Jeremy Hill had to leave for mysterious reasons. Maybe he joined Habitat for Humanity or is helping George Soros or Jimmy Carter or the Koch brothers do some good, maybe the French Foreign Legion, he tells the baby already officially named Anne when she is not Baby Girl, leaning down over Laura and speaking to her stomach, flat as a brick, under the quilt. Then, to Rebecca and to the back of Laura's head, he whispers "Babies love euphemisms." He calls Jeremy by his full name now, Jeremy Hill, as if he were a stranger he must identify for them each time he is mentioned.

He says all these things while reaching to pick up a milkshake he has made for Laura. He already knows where everything is in the kitchen, it is clear, and Rebecca sees small histories of his visits unfolding before her. He holds the glass up high with his left hand like a chalice. Then he cradles Laura's head and persuades her to take a sip, talking into her ear and kissing the air above her head.

After that sip, Laura begins.

"I wanted to start our marriage out right, on a firm foundation of the truth. I wanted to begin with the truth. You know how I am about the truth. If I could just run the world, you know how I have always said this. So, late into the first night on Old Rag where we have been camping many times, just a little way into the woods, just beyond the car, we were setting up in the dark, but we're good at it, so it was no problem. And Jeremy was fine. At first."

Here Laura falters and the tears seep down and she wipes them off with the backs of her hands, the old wedding ring Jeremy Hill found for her in the pawn shop in Richmond glinting on her long fingers, and begins again after another sip of the milkshake from Henry.

"I was pregnant at my wedding. You know that now. And now Jeremy knows it." Laura does not wipe the sheet of tears that run down her face and neck.

"Yes, we know that now," Henry, gleeful, says softly, with pride. "Let's not discuss details now."

His happiness is blinding in the room with the bride propped up, terrible to look at, drinking the power shake he has made her. "The doctors know what to do in cases like this." He grins happily, like a fool. They all smile for different reasons. Rebecca and Weldon are so glad that Laura is alive. They are married by that, united on that, and that is enough.

Laura is composed, if tearful, and intelligent, if incomprehensible, facing a difficult pregnancy and, it seems, a refugee from her own marriage. History is repeating its old terrible self.

She holds Rebecca's hand. Instant sympathy for all mothers including her own, another refugee from marriage, so Rebecca thinks. Rebecca feels more comfortable than she has for years, maybe in her adult life. She is in harmony with her daughter, complete harmony, even if under false pretences. Laura does not know that Rebecca will never leave home again, that Laura's wish has become Rebecca and Weldon's command. Laura feels united with her mother because she has left Jeremy, her husband, following her mother's way of being married. This feeling is, must be, part of what is wrong.

At the emergency room in Richmond, Laura had looked like another young woman found in a Richmond alley, or as if she had been mauled by a bear in the mountains, a possibility which had crossed their minds. She was violently ill as if she had been tossed and slapped around by a bear, one that was not really hungry enough to go to the trouble of tearing away arms and legs.

These facts—"Jeremy blew up the car" and Laura's pregnancy—are the only ones they have to work with. She has not spoken since those outbursts, beyond asking for water and a cigarette. She indicates with a flutter or inclining, a shifting of an arm or finger, what she needs, sipping from a tall glass Henry holds for her. She has indicated that long explanations are coming. She will explain everything. They must be patient.

Jeremy Hill (they are all calling him by his full name now) has vanished. He has not called. He knows that Laura is pregnant and he blew up the car. His parents do not know where he is. Henry has called them now time after time. They are, they say, as baffled as anyone, and they want to come over and sit with Laura. They use that old–fashioned expression that people use for the dead and the sick. They want to bring her honey with the comb in it from their own hives. They will talk about bees, nothing personal, they promise, but their voices fade on the telephone as if the phone itself is growing weaker. Maybe they are driving by, hoping Henry will say that they can come in to sit with Laura.

Henry is willing to talk to the Hills, he says, about bees or planting pines or anything, but they must leave as quickly as they can. Jeremy Hill's friends—their mutual friends, the groomsmen and bridesmaids, even Megan Marshall—do not call. Henry says he has told them to not to for a while. Then he adds that he and Laura were Jeremy Hill's best friends.

Anne Moorefield Hill, Henry predicts, will weigh in at four pounds, two ounces, be delivered by Caesarean section, January third if she does not go full–term to March sixth. He announces the birthday possibilities, and she must be, no, *will* be, willing to wait for Jeremy Hill to visit her as she is sleeping and perfect in the hospital nursery. Henry's prophecy is not an explanation. Laura listens.

Days are passing, and they are waiting for Laura to build up her strength to tell what happened. October appears in the windows, orange and red in the gray rains that try to drain away the colors.

Rebecca has been with Weldon and Gram since the wedding and thinking the way Laura has always wanted her to think: she is where she belongs. At home. At home with Laura and Weldon. Later she will be at home with Anne, her granddaughter, when she is born.

Henry lives there.

Occasionally he leaves to go to his classes or to speak to the professor and get an assignment in order to graduate in December so that he can help send Anne to Paris for her sixteenth birthday, he says.

Weldon and Rebecca are on shifts with Laura, frightened into a semblance of family behaviors (they know to use the plural from the counseling they have gotten for themselves.) They know without being told that they will have to wait for Laura to get on her feet before she can have counseling and before they can find out exactly what happened in the mountains on the wedding camping trip. They must not ask her. Wait. Let days, weeks go by. The doctor used simple words like "Suicide watch." It happens, he said, every day; in fact, it happens every ninety minutes in America.

Laura is frightening—they know it is depression, but it looks like cancer, killing her from inside. They are to go to the emergency room if her blood pressure sinks below eighty over seventy again.

Henry sings about making himself a pallet on the floor. He is as good with Laura as Gram is, as good as Weldon is, who is frightened. Henry considered dropping out of college when it became apparent that something terrible had happened to Laura. They all keep the facts in front of them, all in slow–motion shock: five days after the wedding, the bride comes home. Dazed, ill, scratched and bruised. By the doctor's estimate, three months pregnant. She has lost weight. But here they are and must live their lives somehow.

They speak slowly or raise their voices. They put their hands to their heads as if some thought had hit them. Then, change their minds. They have something to say, but now can't remember it. How is Laura this ten minutes, this twelve minutes? All efforts to soften the shock, to break it up into packages. No topic about them is safe enough for conversation.

Before the wedding, Laura had started Weldon on a running program, she called it. He was, she explained, searching for tone, and at the wedding he was at his best. Those days seem as innocent as light snow falling in April when everyone knows it's not serious. Weldon dancing, drinking but on his feet, with three women there, but under control.

When Laura appeared on foot, five days after the wedding, she "took to her bed" like a nineteenth century neurasthenic. She has stayed in bed. Now, in late October, she has lost her beauty completely; rather, it has condensed itself to a matter of bone structures and shadings of skin. The essentials are there only in absolutes—design of bone and cartilage. There is no fullness, the bloom of her spirit that understood the world, and explained it to anyone who showed interest, has vanished like Jeremy. Everyone knows

what beauty makes men do to each other—launch ships—
throw away an arm in this case. Henry looks at her and
says even her skeletal structure is beautiful, her design is
beautiful, her illness is beautiful, her matted hair is too.
Her shoulder blade sticking out like a small sail is beautiful.
Henry has lost his mind.

How must Rebecca and Weldon talk to these crazy
young people or to each other? For years Rebecca thought
that Weldon was the only really crazy person she knew.
Now she calls it bi–polar disorder. But compared to Laura,
Jeremy and Henry, Weldon is Mr America, mentally. Gram
says of herself that she can feel Alzheimer's beginning its
work.

With the bright, dark hair inherited from her
grandmother, her runner's legs, and her intensity, Laura
was startling at her wedding. Rebecca could understand
Henry's plan to be her second husband even if she had been
outraged by his deliberate announcements at her wedding.
Of course, he did not know that the opportunity would
present itself so quickly. He says this with a careful delight.
He is not exultant: his bride–to–be is ill and the baby, he
does hope that she is his, he says "either/or" "by land or
by sea" "by proxy–sperm or by donor," the baby, his Baby
Girl, has a sixty percent chance of thriving. He refuses to
elaborate and Rebecca and Weldon do not ask questions.
He will say that he thought he had eight to ten years to
court Laura, to wait for her marriage to Jeremy to flounder
and sink. To wait for the second child—the one Laura and
Jeremy would have to save the marriage, it never works—
Emma who would hate homework. He thought he would
have time to build a career in one of his fields, establish
himself, get serious, make him some bucks. Yes, he thought

there would be two daughters whose education he could worry about and plan for. An Anne and an Emma for him to win over and adopt, if not officially then *de facto*–ly. Wrong again, he laughs in an aged way.

It's now late October.

A certain russet landscaped beauty of Rebecca's had appealed to Weldon. "Bridges, winged cheekbones and forehead, high Phoenician ridge, just the topography of the James River basin," Weldon had said about Rebecca twenty–two years ago. They worked on him in the same way that they saw Laura's beauty working on Jeremy and Henry. "Tore me up, tore my heart out of my rib cage." That's exactly what Rebecca had done. Now, Laura had done that to Henry—torn his heart out of his rib cage--he would say to Laura.

CHAPTER FIVE

Rebecca had been wearing a green dress that first night with Weldon. She had washed her hair in the rain water her mother had saved and heated. Then she rolled her hair up in rags.

Rebecca knows that it is Laura's story that must be understood, and not her own, but Laura has turned her face to the wall and stopped living, so Rebecca tells herself her own story, hoping for clues to Laura's silence, for ways to help Laura.

Has anyone heard of rain water and rags for beautiful hair?

Rebecca's beauty lasted just those few hours, and it took only that night to run her life off course, that is, for her to fall in love with Weldon. That night her life shifted its direction and began a glacial movement toward another place. They are living the consequences of that night.

When did Laura's life shift off course? It may have been when she and Jeremy Hill started looking at each other in college or a year later when Henry Moorefield appeared— he would say. It may have been the night when Henry lost his arm. It may have veered off course on the camping trip honeymoon, or the year before sometime, maybe before, the time when Laura, at ten, saw Weldon with the woman, heard Rebecca shoot at Weldon.

Laura will not or cannot speak. She lies in her bed as if she were not four months pregnant with Anne moving in small ways inside her. They all believe that the baby is a girl and that her name is Anne.

On that night with Weldon almost twenty–three years ago, Rebecca did not feel her life changing.

Did Laura feel her life settling its collision course at her wedding or in the mountains or during one of the many times before then when she danced or talked first with Jeremy then with Henry? Or was it one of the many times she watched Weldon and Rebecca come apart? Or that time when she looked through the window and saw her father crying—she said—in the woman we had just met's bed, the van woman?

Who can turn a glacier or steer it toward open land or sea? Away from things it can ruin?

Rebecca stares at the past trying to find hidden things. Laura swimming in the river last summer late at night under the stars burning down on Elk Island. That night Jeremy was working late. Rebecca drove over to the bridge to check on Laura, hoping she would not get angry at her for worrying, hoping she did not hear her car or see the lights. Rebecca has known too many people who went swimming in the James River and had never come home. Laura did get home that night—Rebecca was staying with Weldon for a week because Laura had broken down and cried "Just try a week. For me. You are killing me." Then she had added, "And Gram."

Later, Laura did not say anything about Rebecca's coming to the bridge so she guesses that Laura did not suspect her of driving over there. For once, no suspicion.

When Rebecca thinks of Laura's sleeping around the clock, separating herself from her unborn baby, she tries not to use the word "killing" for what Laura is doing to herself and Anne. Rebecca has come home for good, clearly too late, but now she will not leave, ever. None of them will, can.

Who can use such a word as killer with the word daughter?

Rebecca needs that blowing snow from the glacier of her momentary, long–past moment of beauty to blind her, so she won't do what Weldon's father did with his grandfather's shotgun, or a young husband did to Henry's great–uncle, so she will think of some way to help her daughter and her unborn baby. Wake Laura up, find Jeremy, save the baby.

Henry is still here with them. He has made a pre–birthday cake "with one hand tied behind me so to speak." *ANNE IS COMING* is written in colored letters all squeezed together and taking up the whole cake. He used his mother's recipe for the 1–2–3–4 cake: One cup of butter, two cups of sugar, three cups of flour and four eggs. It's five layers and there are different kinds of icing between each one. Coconut, chocolate, raspberry, hazelnut and seven minute white. Vivian, he says, via phone, was "pressed into service." Mothers are national treasures he says, shaking his head over at Rebecca, balancing the cake to show Laura who does not seem to hear him.

It is late October, Henry has made them appointments to learn about the hospital's neo–natal unit. The doctors are pleased with their responses, but not with Laura's. She is gaining—if one pound can be called a gain. Henry thinks he can hear Anne yawning from inside Laura, and he says she can tuck her chin more gracefully. He says her toes are curling, if she has toes yet. Megan, he reports, has given up on marrying him and that has been a relief, sweet as she is. In fact, he announces, she is pregnant. No, no, not his doing. He heard about it from her very own lips, via phone.

Rebecca tries again to talk to Laura, not just sit in front

of her and feel her skin begin to scorch and curl off in ashes. Not just tell long, pointless stories about Weldon as a young man, Rebecca as a young woman, Laura as a child, but stories that have a point, fables with deep truths.

Laura is far from beautiful now. She looks compressed, condensed. But even with the shadows under her eyes and the fever blisters on her lips, she reminds Rebecca of her old self. She feels a burning in her as she waits for her daughter to say something, to start telling her what happened in that cigarette voice of hers—she smoked even on the way to the hospital. Her voice has always been braided in different chords like a smoker's.

Maybe Rebecca and Weldon should not have built this frame and stone house and lived in the shadow of the Cauthorn's old home place, Gram's house that burned when she was a girl, with the dead generations living here too.

Until that first night in her green dress with Weldon, Rebecca was just a tall, strong looking girl, never close to what Laura is, or what she was before she married. Girls who are beautiful like Laura look the same the minute they get out of bed as they do when they are getting on a plane for London as Laura did three years ago. Hidden lights in their hair and clean lines of bone under their skin twenty-four hours a day.

The green dress was golden–green in the moonlight. It fell over Rebecca's head, a heavy, cool carapace. Shadowed and soft, the way badly polished brass is. It hung from her shoulders in lines that idealized her, she regrets, for Weldon. Twenty–one, still a virgin, going to a party. Weldon had called the day before to ask her to go. He was someone who had registered in her mind as *the man with the dark voice and eyes.*

The marriage was "stormy"; everyone's word, but a better word for it would be "threatening," ready to explode, but holding off. She did threaten to leave him many times. "I cannot be married to you." How many times did she say this!

"You should not be married," she would say stupidly. "You are the perfect son, maybe father, but not husband. You have said it yourself."

His answer was always, "Laura wants us married." They were trapped in wanting to make Laura happy. Laura was listening to them.

He had no idea what living with him, or his family whom he excused by saying that most of them were dead, was like. No idea. They fought without raising their voices. Once Gram left the room and Weldon had a migraine. That was their idea of domestic violence. Rebecca was used to thrown dishes, a hot pan, water. Throwing was what her family did, close to hitting but not quite.

"Unstable." That's what people always called Weldon, but after his students, Kelly Brightley and Dennis Johnson, were killed driving away from school with his permission in his car, he was "diagnosed" and Rebecca started leaving him—this was ten years ago, but five years ago she stayed away with only a few exceptions like the time Laura said she was killing them. Until Laura's wedding.

Weldon asked Rebecca to marry him that night, their first date—it must have been the green–gold dress and rain–washed hair. No one believed Weldon Cauthorn would ever marry. "Unstable, damned likeable, good–hearted, but ruined by the women. There are men who are ruined by women—their mothers, sisters, then all women.

Too handsome, too willing."

He is hell–bent, Weldon says, for Laura to get well, to get out of bed and take her baby away from here when she is born, if she gets to be born, to somewhere where she wants to talk, to live, to explain things again. They cannot worry about the Jeremy or Henry part of the plan.

In the dark car that night so long ago, the glacier shifted a few degrees. Weldon had gone with all the women from here to Richmond, all the ones he wanted. At thirty–four, he was still living at home with all those aunts, the ones he called The Girls. He was drinking like a fish, following in his Uncle Ned's footsteps, keeping three or four women going at once, coming home to his mother and The Girls and his grandmother, Laura's namesake, who worshipped him, but did not love him.

That distinction is Rebecca's mother's: worship is not love. And Rebecca has worshipped Laura instead of loving her.

Weldon wanted to marry because he wanted children, legitimate ones, unaborted ones. He felt that he could reach down into their unformed personalities and make little flowers grow, get them to laugh at the same kinds of things he did, get them to talk to him long before they knew any words. He actually talked about his unborn children—as Henry does—but when he had Laura, he stopped noticing her... maybe it was after she started walking? He was wonderful with her as long as she was a baby, but when she started crawling and then tottering within range of him he withdrew himself from her, not ignoring her, but too aware that she was different, a girl, someone who would be a woman and therefore, maybe, someone he did not want to hurt.

By the time Kelly Brightley and Dennis Johnson were killed in their joy ride in Weldon's car, Laura was looking at Weldon from a very distant place, and it was all his doing.

Henry says that counseling is a growth industry and that they are obligated to support it. That economics lesson, he says, is all he will say about the subject. But it is hard to see how the facts of their lives can be changed by accepting them or looking at them in a new way. Henry has been insisting—he swears a person can change. Yes, he says, Laura can raise Anne with or without Rebecca, Weldon or Jeremy. He is implying that he will be with her, and, of course, with Henry Moorefield, who else, what else is needed? Grandmothers have been invaluable, he tells them, throughout history.

Anne will increase her birth weight miraculously past five pounds, Anne will sleep through the night, as if she had herself a perfect home built on rock, a nicely married set of grandparents, a beautiful mother who may wake up and go to graduate school, a father gone a-hunting maybe, a great–grandmother who lives in a grotto, a one–armed, but wonderful Uncle Henry who hopes he is her father. "Biological, whatever," he says. Henry predicts that it will frighten them to see a baby so happy. They are falling for the atmosphere he is creating.

Why can't Laura recover, leave home after Anne is born, go to a big city, a northern one, and start over? Talk to Jeremy on the phone when she finds him. Explain that she did not want to tell him she was pregnant before the wedding—this is what they gather was/is the problem. Can't they start over? Aren't people reformed alcoholics, reformed wives of suicides, reformed mothers of ruined children, reformed child molesters, reformed murderers?

Henry can continue to wait, as planned, to carry out his original plan to marry Laura after her failed first marriage. So simple, his plan. And the first stage has passed much more quickly than he himself ever dreamed possible.

He takes heart when Rebecca asks him to help her wash Laura's hair and as they work, he asks her to tell him how she and Weldon met and decided to marry. She tells him about the soft green dress, using rain water, and the rags for curling hair. He does smile. Laura remains the same.

CHAPTER SIX

Elk Island is a kind of wilderness. It is, according to many old people, a place they would just as soon not see except in broad daylight. Rebecca's mother's family's home on the Island burned in the 1890's. A house should never have been built there even on that high rising hill on the east end. There are Indian and slave bones there that rattle. People have always said these things and after visiting the island with Laura last summer, Henry said that it was a haunted place. Henry would use that word.

Weldon's students were killed in the fall. Laura was almost the same age as Kelly, and that fall Rebecca began leaving home regularly. Weldon had given Kelly Brightley permission to drive off the school grounds during school hours—a violation of the letter and spirit of all the rules for all schools. He broke the rules, ones he believed in, and the principal had to ask him to resign. Weldon Cauthorn was punished; not as severely, people said, as Kelly and her boyfriend were. Kelly sat up when her mother walked into the hospital room. Weldon and Rebecca walked behind Alma Brightley.

There had been an accident; they should come to the University Hospital; the call about the accident came to the principal's office where they had been summoned when Laura was suspected of being involved in stealing televisions from the elementary school. Everyone knew Laura had not done it—she was twelve—but she let people think, made them think she had organized it. She wanted to be seen as a suspect. Serious discipline problems are handled at the high school by the principal. And the suspicion against Laura was serious and justified. A few years later Laura was in college, miraculously had not failed out of high school as she tried to do, had met Jeremy, but not Henry yet.

Weldon called Rebecca to bring the other car to school and then they drove to Charlottesville to the hospital. The doctors, they were told, were keeping Kelly overnight for observation, but had sent her up to a regular room, 514 East, not intensive care, and not a room off the emergency room. Later that day they learned that Dennis Johnson never made it to the emergency room. They carried him in the ambulance to the funeral home straight from the wreck. The coroner had come to the funeral home.

Kelly smiled sleepily and died, sitting up. Her mother's arms had just reached her and circled her, and her words were already in the air between them, "You are going to be all right." Somewhere in that sentence's time, Kelly died. Her mother caught her as she tilted away from her. She was still treating her daughter as if she were crying about the wreck, the trouble she was in with Mr Cauthorn and Mr Woodson. None of them knew then about Dennis—that he was dead. Rocking and talking to her daughter, Alma Brightley could not take in the new fact.

The nurse rushed over, felt for the pulse at the top of Kelly's perfect leg and began pressing the button over the bed.

They had to back out of the Kelly Brightley's room. They could see before Alma Brightley did, what had happened.

In Weldon's dark car, the Skyhawk—nothing like the Nova

that killed Kelly and Dennis—Rebecca was beautiful in her green dress. That night in her gold–green dress, the wind blew, long breezes drying the cut lespedeza.

After Kelly and Dennis were buried, Weldon wrote to the school board, resigning, as he had been asked to do. The legal implications forced him. The Brightleys did not press charges against Weldon, but they asked that his letter of resignation be published in the Richmond paper and that it include a statement, one they wrote saying that he had "betrayed his profession." Those words had to be in the published letter or they would take Weldon to court. After that, Weldon found a part–time job at the community college.

Weldon had read about cases of burnt and starved children, ones who could be adopted through the mail for seventy–one cents a day. He kept a gallon jar on the table and put seventy–one cents in it every day after Kelly and Dennis were killed. He had started writing to a student in Ho Chi Ming City whose mother wanted them to adopt him. She was an English teacher in the rebuilt city, and when she learned that Weldon taught history, she begged him to take her son. He was college age, actually, graduate school age. They probably would have if Kelly and Dennis had not been killed. When Weldon had to resign after their deaths Rebecca didn't see how they could go ahead with any plans except getting through the next day and then the next one. Vietnam belonged in history books, not in their lives. The war was long over, and they could not be a small Marshall plan.

It was then that Weldon began thinking of suicide

as a practical solution to every one of their problems. Mental and physical ones, as his students wrote on every paper. His life had gotten out of control, another favored expression. But then he started growing mushrooms on water–soaked logs in ponds. The "farm" looked like pens of crocodiles nosed into a trap. He let the ponds grow over when Rebecca left. When they were doing the mushrooms, Gram needed more and more help, but they managed and felt like a family in the effort to keep her from going into a nursing home, the home she stayed in after Kelly and Dennis were killed. Six weeks of hell, she reported, were all anyone needed. Even pedophiles, infanticides would stop if they were sent to a nursing home instead of a jail.

Twenty–two years ago, Rebecca got into Weldon's Skyhawk. A big mistake, she knows now. If she had not inherited Elk Island or washed her hair in the saved rain water, and if she had worn something besides that green–gold dress....

Weldon was thirteen when Rebecca was born. He saw her as what? Possibility? She saw him as an older man, a way to surprise herself, to go to parties, a way to get herself talked about, a trait she has passed on to Laura.

Weldon had waxed his Skyhawk to a negative brightness. Rebecca's dark plum lip gloss matched the car and tasted like it had metallic flecks in it. They were going to a party at the Byrd sisters who owned an old place on the lake, up the river from Elk Island. Weldon wanted a river farm, made no secret of it, and there Rebecca sat, with Elk Island, so to speak, in her lap, in the middle of the river, a lump of gold beside him. He had his grandfather's farm, this one called Cobham, as well as an uncle's, but both farms had creeks, no rivers; in fact, the river was three miles from the houses at the closest points. River land floods so often that it's impossible to farm, but it is still land on the river and far superior to any other land.

So, his attention lights on Rebecca, this young woman, born after his Uncle Ned's war, in a green–gold dress, a girl who owned Elk Island in the James River. Weldon could have resisted her but he did not try, "half–try" the expression is, and she herself, she is sorry and ashamed to say, fell in love that night with herself as the golden woman in the green dress, in love with the way Weldon saw her, her with the rivers in her lap, her in the lap of the rivers— the way, maybe, that Laura fell in love with herself when Jeremy and Henry fell in love with her.

This is all there is to this love story: Rebecca and then Laura falling in love with themselves through the eyes of Weldon and Jeremy/Henry.

Elk Island has one or two good stories attached to it. One is that young Thomas Jefferson used to hunt there. Bear, elk, deer. A hundred years ago, touring parties used to take the canal boats up the Kanawha Canal and stop there for a little taste of wilderness life. They brought cooks who rigged up huge campsites, fires with spits over them as tall as a man, folding chairs. It was fashionable to come to the Island and be scared half to death by the cries of the night herons who sometimes sound as if they are barking or screaming in Icelandic. In their mosquito netting and long linen coats, the Richmonders played at being explorers. The men came out in hunting parties and took back elk antlers.

Rebecca has heard her family laugh at the city people who thought they had been to Africa with Stanley after a few hours at dusk on Elk Island. That was a good use for it. A nineteenth century tourist trap for rich people in Richmond. An old–fashioned theme park. A much better use of it than farming. Richmonders used to shoot stray cows from their touring cars on the one road that crossed from the one bridge to the other, playing safari.

It has never really been farmed. The rich soil is a temptation only to a mad man like Weldon. Rebecca has seen Henry look out of the window toward it—it's three miles north of the stone house with the long windows, straight across the tract of land Continental Can Company bought.

The flood of '71, Agnes, washed out the bridge. The one that's left is almost gone, built in the 1930's. Weldon, that night, looked impossibly wonderful to Rebecca who was one of those girls—they don't exist anymore—who do not suggest at first sight that sex is a possibility.

Weldon, kin to all those aunts, the school teachers, The Sisters. The joke was that they spoke Latin to each other. People claimed they could not understand The Sisters, the English they spoke was so elevated.

Gram brought The Sisters, their ghosts, to them as wedding gifts the day Rebecca and Weldon married. Weldon had his mother and dead aunts who "spoke Latin," he had his polished car, and he had his reputation with women, and a degree in history from the University, and the fact that he was older. These were brought to the marriage. Rebecca brought her youth, and river land, her yearning to be seen as beautiful, desired. A recipe for disaster, a volcano waiting to blow. He had not started teaching then, was still trying to farm, a cross between a dirt and gentleman farmer. He got dirty and could overhaul his tractor engines, and made the place look like something ready for Garden Week. People laughed at him for burying his cows instead of dragging them off to a gully for the buzzards. He trimmed his fences and trained the honeysuckle to grow, it seemed, straight out of the top of fence posts—this really got to people who would drive by just to see his fences which looked like rows of bouquets, wild sprays of flowering honeysuckle coming out of the tops of the posts, not pulling down the wire. Of course, he couldn't and didn't make money training honeysuckle or burying cows.

The night of the Byrd sisters' party, Weldon saw Rebecca in that green–gold dress, thought about owning Elk Island, heard in the birds' screaming the thought that he might make a go of farming the Island. This night is all that there is to the secret dream or madness that he inherited. A few colors, the green and gold, the sounds of the herons and deer, the wet grasses, the old sisters—both the living Byrds and the dead aunts.

The Byrd girls had put in a dipping pool, their word for a rock-lined pool with river bream and minnows in it. They wanted the young people to come stand around it with drinks in their hands. There were wild irises planted in clumps at one end and rock ledges to sit on. They had hired a man and a forklift to come place the big rocks that had been the foundation and chimney for the slave quarters. "We don't like to think of those quarters, so we made something nice out of them," they said, laughing their little birdy laughs. The Byrd sisters wanted to have a wild flower park around the house and dipping pool.

One walk radiating out from the pool would be lined with the Sparrow's Egg Lady's Slipper. They would add the Latin name, and Rebecca memorized it as a souvenir of that night. They said "Lined paths with *cypripedium passerinum*".

That night everything was rushing together: the old Byrd sisters, their dream for a wild flower park around the dipping pool, the new polished Skyhawk, Rebecca's new dress. Fatal beginnings.

Rebecca was flattered to be part of the schemes. That was her dream. That's what women want she would say looking back: to be included. Their beauty, momentary in this case, gets them invited into the madness. She could see herself helping the Byrd Sisters dig up wild flowers, helping lead little tours of their garden, memorizing the Latin names. She could see herself signing the deed for Elk Island over to Weldon Cauthorn and she did in fact later: no one cared what happened to the Island. Who was left in her family anyway? They were dead—her parents and brothers. Fred and Joe died as boys in their wreck, dead drunk in family tradition. Her father drank himself to death. Rebecca would love to drink herself to death and so would Weldon, but they don't feel free to. Laura and Anne would starve. Gram would fade into the dusk out of her window that looks out toward the river.

Weldon kissed her after the party and announced that they would get married. He said she tasted like old pennies. The metallic flecks in the lipstick. He announced their marriage. He did not propose it. He tasted the river land—1600 acres—he had never tasted anything better. Loamy, wild, gamey.

This story of the marriage is getting too far–fetched

and does not make sense even to Rebecca who knows it by heart.

All this is to say that Rebecca's married life began on a high note. She married up, they say in Rivanna. Weldon had better blood, but she had land, free and clear. Very rare in this part of Virginia.

After the party by the pool, they drove to the old bridge, got out of the car and walked across the little river side to the Island. There's the big river side where the bridge washed away and the little river side with the rickety bridge still standing. They walked out across the wet fields where deer were grazing. Do people know that deer shriek when they call each other? They were so quiet and brown in the moonlight and their shrieks were unearthly like men dying on a battle field. Hastings and Chancellorsville may have sounded the way the deer sounded that night. Vietnam flickered in their hearts then died.

Kelly Brightley died without a murmur. Her mother did not cry. Weldon and Rebecca walked backward out of the hospital room when it registered with them. The slackness in Kelly's face meant one thing. Kelly's stepfather, Hill Brightley, a teacher at the school, a good man who had audited Weldon's war course—a first for one teacher to audit another's course in high school—was walking toward them down the hall. When they turned around, he read their faces and rushed by them into the room. The only harsh thing they know about him is that demand he made later for Weldon to write the letter about Kelly's death to the newspaper. There was no sound from the room. The sight of a dead child must be one of a kind. His name connects him to Jeremy in their minds, but they do not know if there any relation, and could not ask.

The hem of Rebecca's green dress was heavy and wet after she waded through the field that runs by the river. The deer were almost baying at the moon. Her lips were metal, like pennies. She felt as strong as a ship, under new power, included in a dream, in an investment, a major stockholder in the East India Company, part of the South Sea Bubble. The "operative" word as Henry would say was dream which rhymes with scheme, he would add. Rebecca does not like to think of how the dress worked. The memory of it can shut out important things. Where in the green–gold–dress story is Kelly's cradling mother or Hill Brightley, rushing by them in the hall? Where is Anne Moorefield Hill?

Hill Brightley walked with great purpose into that hospital room and found Kelly, his only daughter, just dead, propped against her mother.

Laura and Jeremy's wedding was the biggest Rivanna has ever been invited to. They did not complain about driving to New Kent where the Moorefields lived. Gram decided not to go, but she gave Laura her amber necklace to wear.

Dennis Johnson was buried the day after Kelly. Not many people came. Weldon and Rebecca, of course, went. Laura did not go with them.

In her job at the time at the insurance company—Rebecca wrote letters all day to home health care givers who were caring for loved ones at home, or unloved ones. One man was dying alone. He had been evacuated from a hospital in Vietnam, now twenty years ago. Agent Orange. He had married a Vietnamese woman, but couldn't find her when the orders came to evacuate, couldn't get anyone to go find her. They made him leave. Rebecca wanted to tell him about Weldon's plan to adopt Than in one of her letters, but was afraid she would make him worse when he read that they did not adopt Than—couldn't go through it after Weldon's students were killed.

Rebecca sent the veteran a check from the insurance company and included a personal note.

CHAPTER SEVEN

The lightning is playing across the smoked glass of the night sky, cracking it into lumps of quartz. Weldon and Rebecca are awake and looking askance at the show through the low window next to their bed.

This is the big–time leaving, twelve years before Laura's wedding.

"I am leaving. Again. No, what I'm saying is that this time, I will leave for good. You want me to and I will. You can't leave Gram, but I can leave the mushrooms. On Tuesday, I am leaving to take the van back to Jean Warren."

Rebecca knows Weldon is right, so far. She cannot leave home—Weldon's family's farm, the rock and frame house on the old place. "Doing the leaving" was the way Weldon put it the second time. So, he's leaving her with his mother and Laura.

Gram knows her son. She has been through this before with him and she blames herself for the way he is. Sometimes, she gives herself a break and says "circumstances," by which she means Weldon's nature. Weldon will come visit, she is sure; Laura would want him to come. It was the principle of visiting Laura and Gram— they will never mention that he did not talk to them that much when he lived with them—that mattered.

"What about all my notes?"

Weldon had written his thesis on the weather conditions of the Normandy Invasion. Ned's War—Gram's younger brother Ned had been killed on D–Day (Vietnam was Weldon's war, though he did not call it that). Battle plans and maps hung on the wall going upstairs. He drew up lists of veterans and wrote to them to ask for an account of their experiences, but he did not file his stacks of notes. They were not kept in alphabetical order in the boxes stacked to the ceiling in his office. He did not plan to use these notes after he took them, not in his teaching, not for even rereading. He used them to help him live he said.

"What about Jean Warren?" Rebecca is an idiot here, a fool to ask this question an imbecile would not, a baby would not. Later, she hears him moaning in his sleep, more company than when he is awake because he has stopped talking to her, again, except to ask her questions. The question about his notes is one he has asked her several times since she followed him to Jean Warren's house the week before.

That two hundred mile trip to Elkton had not gotten them where they were going—the funeral of Rebecca's ninety–seven year old cousin—and when they got home and went to bed, Weldon told her Tuesday was the day he would leave. Again. Halfway to Elkton, the head gasket had blown on the station wagon and left them stranded at Warren's Service Garage. Laura was ten when they drove toward Elkton.

Everyone said Rebecca was the difficult one, the half–crazy one, that Weldon had a lot to put up with. The truth was that all he did to attract women to him was allow them to love him on his terms, something Rebecca had done and was doing, but there were women who were willing to take him as he was—crazy, poor and married. To be available is a rare thing, but no one seems to know it. What love meant to both Weldon and Laura was simply being available— for Weldon, that availability included sex. Rebecca is the one who sees love as more of a multiple choice test; eliminate all the wrong answers and hope the last one is right. Weldon would say that all the answers were possible. The vodka—he switched from bourbon to vodka—helps lower any resistance for guarding his availability, and the Chesterfields he smokes make him more attractive in an old movie way. That's the power Weldon has. Even now after having lived with him for five centuries, Rebecca wants to smoke because he does and Laura does, Rebecca is sure.

Jean Warren's husband drove Laura and Rebecca over to his house from the garage because he kept saying "something must have happened to Jean and your husband. They are taking too damn long. The damn thing probably wouldn't start which does happen, can happen, and most likely did happen. Vans are funny. Very funny bitches." He laughed at the inevitability of things, and Rebecca did too.

They pulled into his yard.

"Just run up to the door," he said to Laura, not realizing that no one told Laura to do little things as if she were an old fashioned child and not a kid of the modern era, "Just bang on it while I turn around. See if there's any trouble. Jean may be fixing your old man a glass of tea, I don't know."

It was not tea.

Laura banged on the door, bored. She kept on. "Run around back. Jean may have turned on the tube." Laura walked around the corner of the yellow house and did not come back. Then Rebecca went around and found the back door locked up, the sounds of the television coming through the air conditioning, a loud window unit set in a window with no curtains. She turned around to see Paul

Warren walking toward the back door.

Laura turned and ran straight away from the window, down the hill behind the house, and then she disappeared.

"Your little girl just saw something, I bet, something you would not want her to. You wouldn't want to see it yourself, if you climbed up and looked over my ac unit. So, I think it's best that we hightail it out of here, or excuse my French, haul ass while someone I know and someone you know get their act together, that's my way of saying get their clothes on."

Then the owner of Warren's Garage in his adult way, expecting Rebecca to act the same way, walked back to the truck and waited for her to follow which she did.

They found Laura by cutting through a back street, and made her get in, all hot and white but not crying. Rebecca did not ask her anything. They waited for almost an hour back at Warren's Garage until Weldon showed up with Jean Warren. Then they drove the Warrens' van home.

In the hopelessness of trying to keep Weldon's attention, Rebecca had gone through phases, what she called her "projects" so often that everyone felt free to offer this diagnosis: unstable. Her projects gave Weldon more license, more women. A man with a difficult wife deserved any help he could get. Rebecca could see her own interest tapering off, evaporating from each venture almost as it began—jogging, the kiln, photography, now the mushrooms—and hear the ugly, flat sound of: "unstable." Weldon's obsessions with Ned's War or Vietnam, on the other hand, never wavered. The notes he took sat in boxes softened by mildew. He never used the letters from the veterans either—he asked the veterans to write about what happened to their families back home, not about the war.

Some new woman's with Weldon, and Rebecca's going off—this was the county's take on them. Rivanna knew Weldon and Rebecca, make no mistake. The county might look isolated, wooded, (mixed hardwood and pine), bears seen at the dumps every year, deer coming into range of the charcoal grills, but it was not backwoods. There were mud rooms and cathedral ceilings, flagstoned backyards; heat pumps to make woodstoves a nice thing, not necessities, vcr's, cd's, microwaves, satellite dishes, a few vinyl–lined swimming pools.

Rebecca, they said, not without some affection (she knows that) was crazy. Had to be, given her family. They said this every time she started a new project or job. Why shouldn't she be, married into that Cauthorn family, not to mention her own family, the Carrolls. When she said things, she should be listened to as if she were making sense. Sympathy, if nothing else. Starting a new project was cheaper than a shrink, though she had tried those too, later, not that anyone else had ever tried one. Work made sense. What's Rebecca up to now, they asked, tolerant and interested and even "supportive," a word Rivanna had started using lately, picked up from television talk shows.

Sometimes they slipped when they saw her. Often she looked as if she had just gotten in the door from a windstorm, but flying hair was becoming a popular hair style and she did not care that at thirty she was getting toward the age when, in Rivanna, women cut their hair and all wore more of less the same permed hairdo. When she was first married, she pulled all her hair back into what she called a psyche knot. Weldon had liked it. Then he liked her wild hair and called her for a few weeks his French Lieutenant's woman. But he knew that he liked short hair too. He didn't even lower his voice when he complimented women's hair—that's a Roman boy's cut, I believe, he would say. The Rivanna women loved him for calling their short haircuts Roman boys'. Weldon is Ned all over again, they said; then added, *almost* Ned Nelson all over again.

Weldon knew that Rebecca's witchy looks owed a lot to his just–as–soon habit, any–woman–every–woman way of thinking. Gram would tell how Ned used to talk to Weldon, cutting his eyes from the mirror hung on the back porch to catch Henry's attention. Ned was getting ready for one of his "assignations." "Short, thin, fat, or tall, Ole Ned Nelson loves them all."

Weldon had understood, Gram claimed, what Ned meant, watching the razor go up the lifted chin. Ned made lather with the brush from the Old Spice mug all over his face and neck. His shirt hung down from his belt, a towel was draped over his shoulders, his hair curling down the back of his neck. Ned had ruined Weldon. That's one theory.

Weldon absorbed the wisdom of Ned's views of women—there was something to wonder at in every one of them. Rebecca was sorry Ned had been killed because his death had arrested Weldon's development,—a phrase she had picked up from the air, it was everywhere. Weldon would just as soon have been at Warren's garage watching the mechanic take out the thermostat on a wrecked Bronco as at the funeral in Elkton as in Jean Warren's bed. Martha Travis and Liz McClanahan are waiting in the future. Rebecca is usually there if all else fails.

Weldon decided to marry Rebecca of the green–gold dress. His feeling was that he'd just as soon be married to her who seemed to know already what their life would be like. He felt sorry for her, sometimes, for the energy she spent on making things seem new, on attracting his attention. He didn't understand why she didn't take the world, and him, as they were. His study of war was his way of studying things as they were, are and will be. He quoted Pope, giving the wrong emphasis to "is"—"Whatever is *is*, right?" turning it into a rhetorical question, not an equation of is–ness with rightness.

The rain is driving down on the old slate roof. Silence, then a roar of rain. In the silences, Rebecca hears a clicking that she knows is Duchess shaking her head and scratching. The dog can snap her ears so fast it sounds like a light switch being flipped on and off. Understanding what is actually happening gives her some pleasure–things that Weldon marveled at for actually happening were messages to her. The sounds from the bedrooms tell her where Laura is sleeping. One bed has boxed springs and one the old steel springs left from Weldon's college years. Laura hardly ever sleeps in the same bed two nights in a row. Rebecca does not hear one rusty swenge of the springs and knows that Laura has left the house again to ramble around in the woods.

She knows that Laura is ashamed of Weldon and her for their inability to live together, to be married, ashamed for their natures. Laura thinks that Rebecca is a liar—that her projects are lies, false. She is phoniness personified, Laura has said, and cannot distinguish between hope and lies. She does not care about the hard work her mother does. When Rebecca fails, it means that the "truth" has been uncovered. Weldon's lies are more simple ones, understandable, calls of nature.

At ten, Laura is filled with despair about the possibility of having to live with her parents as they are. She leaves the house and goes out on the Island. Roaming the house at night, changing beds, she is practicing the just–as–soon ways of her father. She tells Rebecca "it fries my eyeballs to live with you two, no offense."

Rebecca remembers feeling that way about living at home with Austa Ilene and Irving—her parents—though she didn't think of fried eyes. Once her brothers, Fred and Joe, scoured the lime walls of the old parlor with her, and she felt sick, flushed with rage, and the many times Austa Ilene would ask Irving "You are not drinking, Irving, are you?" Rebecca did think of dying, either as the one causing death, getting to be the killer or as the quiet, done–wrong–to dead person. This is when she shot the gun in the direction of Weldon, when she was thinking of death in the getting-to-be-the killer way.

Laura dyed her hair and cut it outrageously and dressed like the pictures Weldon had collected of the refugees after the war. At other times, she looked like a member of a London rock group.

Protected by his just–as–soon–this–as–that vision, Weldon enjoyed Laura from a distance. "No chance am I going to be the child you wish I were," Laura says to them. Weldon is delighted but does not say anything.

Rebecca had not been able to change Weldon's habit of inventorying the universe. Weldon looked out into space, she said, to collect odd information. She tried to shame him by telling him that children read clouds for fun before they grow up, but then they put away childish things. He read the house, the rain and lambs quarter in the garden as auspices, not of anything specific, but just for the pleasure of reading. Like his note-taking on D–Day and the fall of Saigon. He was a cloud reader, she said, but he just read the cloudy suffixes, the "ed's" and "tions," not the words that gave the message any meaning.

The same thing about his letters from the veterans. He must have received hundreds and what did they add up to? They were just notes leading nowhere. Rebecca was the one who had to make out the message. That's why he loved her, he explained when he was speaking—she knew that he loved "cloudy suffixes."

Suffixes, not words, were what they were living by. In their last fight about his cloudy suffixes, Weldon tried to explain himself by saying that every silk on an ear of corn represented a kernel, but it was beyond anyone's power to connect a silk and a kernel, so a person, himself for instance, had to read the silk, the kernel, the cloud.

Rebecca just looked at him. He didn't think she would divorce him because of cloudy suffixes. She would have preferred him drunk—alcohol ran in both families—to being what he was, and he was drunk often. This silk and kernel eye for detail had passed itself off as a genius for detail, but as she pointed out, it didn't help the marriage or the tax bill. Rebecca wanted him to connect things, have payment books with nothing but stubs to rifle through. She wanted him to exert himself against fortuities, not just record them.

After their worst fight when he had held her arm up in the air, ignoring the gun in her hand, he heard her on the phone saying that she was sure he was ready to be taken away, but it was too expensive to go in for treatment and that as she understood it, she needed three people including a doctor to sign him into a hospital. She could forget the doctor, he had said as she tried to put the phone down. She had the gun, but he was the crazy one. Say what?

The marriage was a car on black ice, a glazed incline; then a deer leaps onto the hood and crashes through the windshield, paws the couple to death, the couple who were sliding toward death maybe anyway, sideways down the icy hill, so shooting the gun was not as big a deal as it would be with other people. Weldon never mentioned it afterwards. Gram either.

So Rebecca was running the mushroom operation. For a while, Weldon was doing the heavy and absurd work, unloading the pulp wood into the pond, standing in the muck and implanting the fungi under the bark that in three months sprouted out into big thumbs of speckled mushrooms that the Asian restaurants in D.C. wanted. It was not as crazy an idea as it had sounded when she first told Weldon what she wanted to do, what she was, in fact, going to do, but it was a far cry from what he had expected her to do: garden, freeze and can vegetables, rear five children. They were so deep in debt then, and she could not leave Gram and forget the mushrooms. The fork lift, timber jack and truck had been as far as the bank would go with them and fifty thousand dollars for a mushroom farm in the middle of corn country was what they owed.

Weldon wanted the Island to be his Kansas, fields of eight–foot hybrid corn grown for DeKalb.

The cousin's funeral in Elkton, North Carolina, came just at the right time. Some people even die considerately. They needed a break from the hard work, a day trip to get away from the thoughts of not being able to make the installment payments on the equipment for the mushrooms. They were happy, for them, in their way, to go to North Carolina to a funeral. This trip would let them rest.

Rebecca had been the first one to notice when the heat light blinked over the speedometer. They had just whizzed over a dried up gulch called Difficult Creek on the interstate and there were cardboard signs announcing ten miles along the way that Mt. Laurel was having its First Annual Cantaloupe Festival. Weldon added these things to his store of useless information. More cloudy suffixes.

The blown head gasket kept them in Mt. Laurel all afternoon as the funeral went on two hours away. At Warren's Garage, Weldon and Laura were happy watching the fat man with a cigarette behind his ear rotate tires and lower an engine into a bug that had just had surgery to make it into a pickup truck with huge rear wheels. They acted as if they were on a field trip studying small town mechanics.

By four–thirty, the afternoon had worn them down. Their funeral clothes had pickle juice and catsup and slashes of tire marks where they had leaned on tires stacked along the wall.

Laura wouldn't eat meat, having been a vegetarian for three weeks (though she eyed the bacon cheeseburger). She filled up on fries. Weldon did an inventory of the guns, flags and girls without underpants on calendars in the garage. Rebecca found a car and sat in it so she could balance the checkbook and clean out her pocketbook.

At five o'clock, Jean Warren came over to Rebecca and leaned on the parked Toyota.

"You could drive my van home. It's doing nothing but being here trying to get itself sold for me."

"When will my car be ready?"

"Couldn't say, but you are welcome to my van. I just use it to pull my boat, and like I said, it's at home just soaking up the sun." Her coveralls were unbuttoned enough to show a halter top under them. JEAN WARREN was written across her back. "Your husband could drive it back to me. When he got a chance."

Laura was thrilled with the thought of them in a van, maybe with muted metallic scenes of Hawaii, the mountains and surf separated by a swirling hula dancer. She could creep into its sky blue interior fixed up like a doll's house for heavy drinkers, the ice chest and bar bolted down, the swivel stools covered in velour. "We'll look rich and evil," Laura whispered to Weldon, who told Jean Warren he would drive home with her right then and pick up the van.

Weldon took the keys and listened to the instructions about the gears locking. Jean Warren knew about stranded families, she had seen a few in her time. She offered a few words of comfort about the funeral they were missing. Weldon was listening hard to Jean Warren, whose eyes were like a cola just poured, still fizzing. Her voice was carbonated too.

"You just ride with me home to pick up my van and I'll let you have it to drive home, then you can bring it back next week when we have your wagon fixed. How's that?"

Weldon lit up a Chesterfield and Jean Warren asked if she could have one. Jean Warren let her husband do the talking while she got the keys to his car from the office and came back out.

"Those heads are liable to blow any time at all. I've learned that little lesson. Last month, my brother–in–law just blowed his sky high, and he was driving his car off the lot. He come by here, I mean, had the thing towed here from Plainview where he bought it, for me to tear down the engine, brand new, and that's what I found when I got in there. You could have fooled me. You don't expect a head gasket to act up in a new car. Yours is a different story. I expected it in a way if you know what I mean. I could tell when you drove in real slow, it was real heated up, and I could see this car's been drove more than a hundred thousand. Head gasket. My brother–in–law said if he didn't have bad luck, he wouldn't have no luck at all, but I guess that's a good thing for all us to remember. You can't tell a thing about an engine now. They can blow any day of the week. Right off the lot, too. I'm almost afraid myself to go out on the highways and not because of drunk teenagers either. But like I said, you feel free to take the van and bring it back when you want. We'll have your little number fixed by next Tuesday, I am positive."

Three hours later Jean Warren's van ploughed windy furrows up the interstate drinking a gallon of gas every five or six miles. Rebecca sits high above the engine, a kidnapped diplomat's wife. Laura rides, a child movie star, one with leukemia. She does not speak all the way home. Weldon fixes the locked gears under the hood twice.

Saturday night in the hard rains, the van gleamed under the spotlights burning down on their new sign that said Cauthorn's Mushrooms. On the sides of the van, the scenes of island beauty were dark.

Weldon took the van back on Tuesday. He did not mention Jean Warren. He came home on Wednesday.

How would Rebecca have lived without Weldon? She knows many wives who continue their marriages long after the men have left.

Riding in the van, she felt weightless, beyond gravity, and in the company of the clouds, nosing down toward earth out, the sun coming through the tinted windows warming her over the air conditioning.

Going to the funeral in North Carolina had seemed like a good idea, a forced mini–vacation from the damp heat of mushroom farming where they shipped out crates of fungi to become garnishes and pale flavors reminding Cambodian and Vietnamese communities in Washington of home. Rebecca, another project underway, was creating a local market in Rivanna which had never thought of mushrooms except as first, Campbell's soup and later, mushroom pizza. Now the neighbors were making mushroom quiches. She might put on a mushroom festival one year soon like the Mt. Laurel one for cantaloupes.

The trip and the borrowed van with Jean Warren's nail polish bottle stuck down in the drink holes in the dash bruised Rebecca's faith in herself to have the energy and power to launch, to catapult the Cauthorns as a family into their futures. Rebecca had given up as they drove home in the van to Gram waiting for them. Any efforts to recall the green–gold dress or to imagine her eyes as blue stones, her nose as high and arched, her hair as floating on salty air, her daughter as a honor roll student not the furious ten year old who has announced that she is quitting school and later will go to the community college if she goes to college which is for losers anyway.

Duchess is clicking her ears and Laura's bed is not whining as Weldon stares out of the window, his back to Rebecca who knows he thinks the music of the stone house is beautiful, broken and in pieces at the moment because of his little slip-up with Jean Warren, the van woman, but he does not suggest anything, no cause and effect, not a word about the marriage cracking up in his bed. Rebecca knows Weldon will drive the van back on Tuesday, and deep in herself, she knows that he will come back home, and that she will have to do the leaving. Weldon will have coffee with Jean Warren, then something else after the sandwich and beer.

CHAPTER EIGHT

Laura knows her life is wrecked, but she does not want to know it. Classic denial—she knows all the definitions of her condition. She craves sleep not for escape, but for the sense of order the dreams bring her. Dreaming of revenge, an organized massacre, one planned by experts, born killers who look like professors, she avoids murdering her family, her unborn new daughter, herself.

Sleeping and dreaming are her defenses "against self slaughter and massacre," as Henry would say, and as he partly understands. But she wavers and moves in close to taking herself out, slipping off and forgetting everything she has explained about life when she is awake.

She remembers she has pills (a gun would be impossible to get now). It would be easy with the pills—they are over a year old, the ones she saved from friends at college. But where are they? To find them, she will have to get up and look, make a phone call, be normal.

Killing will be a problem, and it's not having them dead that will help. She wants acknowledgment, a nod, a look that says she has been driven by a tsunami–like thing into a wall, she has crashed into a log truck, run up under it. Her life is smeared on the highway. She wants them all— Rebecca and Weldon who are at the heart of it, Jeremy wherever he is, Henry who brought all of this down on himself, was available as a sperm bank—to see that she is trapped in an open field, the spotlighting hunters catching her in their telescopic lens waiting for her to run so there will be some fun to the shot.

She does not want to go on living in this way, this new way: In bed. The thing wrong with her life is that it is not her life any longer.

She never imagined that Jeremy would go crazy and blow up the car when she told him about the baby and Henry—there is no baby, evidently, unless Jeremy says there is, unless it is his baby, and for Jeremy, there is no Henry in her life except as a joke, *their* friend on Jeremy's terms, nothing else, the talker, the wild man, the best man, the fraternity brother who went too far and exposed them all to trouble.

When Henry loomed up that night in the mountains in Laura's talk, Jeremy ripped off his shirt, soaked it in gasoline and stuffed it down in the gas tank of the car. She finishes telling him, explaining about autonomous sex and the ultimate test of love. Thinking out loud to her new husband, the man she loved and trusted to always do what she needed doing, no questions, the man, Jeremy, she trusted to help her carry out the plan: she, that is, they, she and Jeremy, would have Henry's child—no, Henry did not know she was pregnant—and Jeremy would repay Henry for the loss of his arm by accepting the baby as his own. Jeremy would offer his first born, in a way, to Henry, meaning that Henry got to have their first born, Jeremy must know it and carry the fact of it bravely and see it as balancing what had happened to Henry because of Jeremy. It took a long time to say it all, to complete the several ways to get to the point of how they were balancing the books and making things right.

Finally, after a long time of staring up into the pale night sky, Jeremy answered her. They were lying side by side in the warm dark.

"So, what you are saying is that I am giving you to Henry? Forget the baby. You are the one I know, and you are saying that my bride, the woman I have just married a few hours back, is not mine. Not really mine. That's what all this talk boils down to."

Laura is explaining these things again. She wants Jeremy to go in with her on this: she was actually helping them all. She is a surrogate mother, in a way, she is offering Henry compensation for what he had lost. A baby for his arm. Laura's baby at that. Because of his so—called love, all his talk about her and how much he loved her, it is perfect. Jeremy's compliance and goodness, those will balance the scales. All will turn out fine, just fine.

Laura remembers weaving her fingers together over her almost flat stomach, happy—for the last time—that the truth had been told. The wind rose in the trees and the deer adjusted themselves in their barrows.

It was late that first night after their three hour hike away from the camp site and back, and she has been talking for so long. She thinks Jeremy is getting up to start a fire for them. They can hear the deer.

They had had sex. The usual good time. The deer were settling down after grazing, into the big cradles of limbs in the woods. Jeremy had told her he could hear them just before she began telling Jeremy what he had to know, and had to know on their first night of the honeymoon.

It does not work, to say the least. Jeremy loses it, then she does. Everything is ruined, up in smoke. Married for what? Not twenty hours.

Laura has read about women who arise as if from a refreshing sleep and kill their children and husbands, and so, though she would like to kill, she is afraid to wake up and kill herself and the baby in her, all in one shot or gulp of water and pills.

Jeremy is not here anyway, so she can't kill him. He may be dead by now. He had screamed that she had killed him.

She has read accounts, long studies making clear why murders were inevitable, not shocking really when you knew the histories, all the husbands and mothers with the guns or gun substitutes.

Laura avoids assigning herself the job of killing herself and the baby who seems to give a tiny, tacit permission: "I am not much, hardly here. Go ahead." Her—she knows it is a girl—embryo fingers must be like punctuation marks. It would be much better to kill herself than everyone else, and she is trying to protect everyone else, but it is slow, her dying. No wonder hunger strikes don't intimidate governments. They can last forever. Sleeping herself to death may be faster than starving.

Laura, even in her dreams, cannot destroy Jeremy and Henry, so she concentrates on Rebecca and Weldon who turned her into an explaining machine because everything they did, their coming and going, needed an explanation.

She could get up, boil an egg, drink juice, go running, start loving and planning for the baby, learn to love her before she's born, teach her to read by the time she's twenty months (she has read about babies who read big signs on refrigerators) then go live in a city, get a job, day care, learn a new kind of life with her by then beautiful, big, tall, healthy daughter. Maybe she will be an athletic daughter who will make 1600 on the SAT's and win scholarships. Laura could send clippings about her awards back to Weldon and Rebecca. Gram will be dead, but "still around" as she calls her dead husband and friends now. Laura could do these things, ordinary life could triumph if she took the first step toward it. She knows these things, but she can't give up the life she had in her mind with Jeremy. Her plans to balance the scales of what happened to Henry with what Jeremy would do to make it up, the right things, to adjust the way the picture of their lives was hanging on the wall, are not working. Tested, tried and true Jeremy: she had been certain that he would welcome the baby, because it was Laura's baby, and after knowing about the coming baby, he would never let anything else get to him or shake the foundation of his marriage. When he understood that the baby was Henry's, or might be, he would be relieved, glad when she explained everything, in a deep, deep way. It would settle the account of the night on the tracks, of the night when Henry was almost killed by the train, and should by all accounts have died. Jeremy could be freed of guilt, then, by taking on Henry's baby—if the baby were Henry's. Babies cost a hundred thousand dollars now, middle class babies. Jeremy would work himself to death, happy to pay for all the things the baby needed. Jeremy could stare at trains again. They could face anything else that life had up its sleeve. Her plan. Pulverized.

Anyway, the gun for a killing spree would be hard for Laura to reach, up high on the rack in the kitchen. Some of Weldon's grandfather's guns were saved, they think, when his Great Aunt Lou turned over the lamp in 1911 and burned up the house, but where are those guns now? Weldon doesn't like guns, never had a gun in the house— except that shotgun on the rack in the kitchen, the one that was actually rescued from the fire, the L.C. double barrel one that Rebecca shot into the air over Weldon's head.

No one knew the gun was loaded—that's the official

SUSAN PEPPER ROBBINS

story. Laura has heard several versions of the story from Henry who had heard it from her back when all was better. Now, she hears him saying it back to her as she lies in bed, but as if she were sitting up and riding in his Thunderbird, and she were explaining her parents to him and his parents to him, in the years before the night on Island and in the river. Henry is telling her her family's story now, a ploy, a trick to catch her attention and make her want to correct him when he deliberately makes a mistake. He thinks that the depression that has settled in her brain and deep into her body is something like a worst case attention deficit problem. HE can snag a piece of its slimy dead fish skin with a sharp hook, make her mad that he has appropriated her life, her family, her impossible parents, her shooting, murdering mother. So Henry thinks the story he is telling now will have a shock therapy value, this more recent one, a true story, about Jeremy's showing up.

"Good God, Laura, we were almost killed by that maniac. Jeremy had his knife, and he kept his hand on it while he talked to us, at us. He told us—listen up, my darling—how you rammed his car into a tree and cracked the manifold so that it caught on fire when he was driving it to a mechanic in Waynesboro. He said the car blew up and that he barely got out and when he went back to get you, you were gone.

"His mind is messed up pretty bad, but having the knife, when he told all these lies, he had the floor, so to speak, and we let him rant and rave on to his heart's content.

"Weldon saved our lives, really, he did. He walked across the kitchen as if he were headed toward the coffee pot, then stepped up to the gun on the rack over the mantle. Your old man, your Weldon, the man with his marriage and his love life, his girl friend he asked you to lie about all those years of your blasted childhood (was her name Jean Warren? Isn't she the one you looked through the window at, saw them flagrante, and fled yourself, all of ten years old? See, my darling, how well I know your life, I do, I do... not to bring up my I–do plans, which are on the back burner for now, for now). I do know your charming and unreliable dad and his loving but unstable wife, your mom, and I know your dad's dead students, Kelly Brightly and Dennis Johnson. See, I know their names and where they are buried and how old they would be and what they would be doing, yes, that father of yours, the day your present husband came to call, the father we call Weldon, walked over to the gun, leaned toward it, then tore it off its rack, whipped around as if he were in an old western movie and told Jeremy to leave and never set foot on Cobham again.

"Those were his words. 'Set foot!' I never thought I would hear those words in my life. It was pure heroics, it was past cool, way past. And your terrible husband, your present husband until we can get things straight with an attorney, did just that—left, exited the scene, disappeared. Mid–sentence. But it was not over, not then, not yet.

"Jeremy Hill went out the back way, knowing the house as he does, picked up Weldon's chain saw and pulled the rope once into action and took down a row of the Lombardy Poplars Rebecca had planted on one of her returns—I think it was a weekend in 1988.

"'Tell Laura I will be back.'" So, I am telling you. I did not say a word at the time. I was biding my time as you know, making myself useful. I tell this story of your husband's violent rampage to wake you up to the reality of the situation, the situation in which I am waiting for you as your Prince Charming—not too far off as a soubriquet.

"Well, back to the action–adventure. Gram was not in the kitchen and Rebecca sat as still as stone during the attempted murder, as I call it. I was there, as I have said, my neck several inches from the knife, my heart in my throat, I will admit, because I did not, repeat, *did not*, want to die just then and on Jeremy Hill's schedule. I was very relieved when he grabbed the chain saw and put up his knife. I did not think he would massacre us with the saw, I must say I did not think that he would, and when he knocked out five of the poplars and threw down the saw still running and skittering all over the ground, I knew we were safe, shut of him forever. How could he ever come back after such a display of madness? How could you take him back? I think there is a law against reconciling with a criminal. I'll look it up.

"I was saving myself, my life, for Anne, as you know; my father–self. The other parts of me are yours if and when you should ever want them, my darling Laura, Rose of my Heart. Jeremy Hill did curse me, but as I say he did not kill me for which I am grateful to him, because I could see murder spelled out in those pale green eyes and across the bridge of his nose. In fact, he said he wanted to kill 'a sorry one–armed bastard who was in the room' but he would not, at least not now. I do not know what stayed his hand. Maybe good sense, maybe knowing that he would go to jail, the chair maybe, in this political climate. Because I am sure he thought that he would take us all out and then himself. I don't know if he thought he would kill you. All I know is that we were preserved. Weldon could not have shot him before he stuck that knife in good, deep into my unprotected neck. Weldon says so himself. Rebecca did not flinch and never took her eyes off him. It was family violence at its most celebrated—a gun, a knife, then the chain saw, a deranged groom, a father, a mother, a rejected (sort of) suitor. I enjoyed it a little at the time, but far more afterward, and now in telling you as therapy—truth serum, an amytal interview, though I am, as usual, doing all the talking. Everything in retro, I say, as you have heard me report, my own Heart's Ease."

Laura does not flinch, like her mother, or move, but she takes in Henry's account of Jeremy's visit. She had heard a door slam in the mid–afternoon that day and fierce voices, and the next week in the unseasonable, freakish snowfall, she had seen footprints outside her window. She waited up the following night, pretending to be sleeping instead of being asleep. After midnight, when Rebecca had just left her room, Laura walked over to the window. The prints led up to her low sill, walked ten or so steps back and then retraced themselves back toward the woods sloping downward to the river three miles away. She did not say anything the next morning because she had not said anything about the footprints the first night. The shadows from the trees lay sharp as knives on the bright snow. The footprints stepped away between the crisscrossing shadows as the wind bent the trees. Then the snow was gone.

Henry is sure that he is helping bring Laura back into her life by telling her stories, updating her on their daily lives. He uses Gram's stories and Anne's pre–natal life as bright beads and whiskey, throwing them down, trading. Jeremy Hill's visit was his best card and he brings out details from it to keep her attention—that is, to see a brief, tensile shadow cross Laura's face, a sign to him of her connection to him: to life.

To Laura, Anne does not feel like a person yet, not a real baby, not her baby, not yet. Nothing has worked out the way she planned it. She cannot believe what has happened. That Jeremy could not take what she had to tell him, that it did not make him stronger, more in love, that he has come here with a knife, that he has come to her window in the snow like an animal or a murderer!

Weldon never hunted, he said, because he had cleaned too many squirrels and rabbits brought home by his grandfather and Uncle Ned. He had bitten down on too many pieces of shot in squirrel stew.

Henry doesn't keep guns. He was a bow hunter and he had high tech bows hanging from pegs he drove in the walls of his dorm room. He was impressed with Weldon's handling the rifle when Jeremy came in with the knife; he looked like a life–time hunter. Gram doesn't know what happened to the other old guns saved from the fire, and if she did know, she would not tell. She knows what thoughts a gun puts in a man's mind, as she has said many times, but Henry has gently told her that modern warriors do not need guns, they hunt with cars, the weapons of choice. A cross between a tank and a missile. "While I drive, I hunt, figuratively, atavistically. Two birds with one stone."

In her sleep, Laura is seeing the simplest, most efficient solutions to her problem. In her sleep, she is free to turn on herself, starve herself down to a branch, a piece of broom sedge. Testing Jeremy's love has ruined her life—getting pregnant and marrying Jeremy. The baby makes Laura a what? Something she hates, something like a mother, like a Rebecca who quits, who leaves, who must be placated and begged to stay. If Jeremy loved her, he would have let the train hit him, would have taken her night when she had sex with Henry in the river, taken it all in stride. The information about Henry and the river does not automatically make Henry the father because she and Jeremy had sex too, not in the river but where they could. It is Jeremy who has given/thrown Laura away, failed the test, forsaken the baby—maybe his—and ruined their love and marriage forever.

Asleep, Laura can tolerate what has happened. Awake, she is a killer. She can kill (not with a gun) her baby and her family and Henry too, and go scot free by refusing to get up, to eat, to reach for the baby. A young woman who made a mistake, had chosen the wrong man to marry, had the wrong baby with the wrong man, then dies. On her back, floating away, she is relieved to be sleeping, this thin, unreal sleep that flattens out her life into charts and graphs, presenting simple alternatives: Suicide—murder.

In July, that now long ago July before the sleeping, the wedding, all of it, Henry had said he was coming by that night. They sat on the porch. There was the wedding coming up, there were Weldon and Martha Travis and Rebecca to talk about, Rebecca would go to the wedding with Weldon—that is follow him in her car—the caterers, the roses at the Moorefields.

A baby is a baby, period. Ordinary as babies are, born every second, they are grenades. More like bombs. Hiroshimas happen every time a baby is born, every time a woman discovers (the right word) that she is pregnant. Laura knows all the stories about girls and babies, terrible ones about babies left in dumpsters, babies left in motel rooms.

Laura knew that Rebecca was a little bit pregnant with her when she and Weldon married. That kind of wedding rushed into the parlor hardly dusted with some forced forsythia and japonica, a cake baked that morning, seems happy and safe to Laura. Sweet and old fashioned. Same old, same old problems. Henry would have said before he knew about Anne, look, it's the nineties, girlfriends, all that baby/father thing is dead, all over except for a few little brush fires. He meant abortion. Go get one. Then he heard that he was going to meet his Annie, his Anne. Just like the ads against abortion say. He's a "personalized pro–lifer" now. He calls himself a "lifer" and he's happy with the prison sentence. "Pour it on," he says with every bobble of Anne's fist–sized head felt through Laura's skin and Gram's quilt, every ballerina droop of her feet and wrists, every anticipated diaper change in March, now his favorite month.

Laura does not listen. She is dreaming her dreams about last July.

Laura running down the steps of the porch. Rebecca and Weldon do not hear her. They are having a date, watching television, a rented movie. Weldon has gotten his favorite, one that has everything he said—the mafia, holocaust, Everglades, drug rings, a corrupt senator, and best of all, a renewed love. Weldon invited Laura to watch it with him and Rebecca, and Henry too. She said maybe. Jeremy is working a double shift. Gram does not hear Laura scream at eight o'clock.

Henry follows her in his old Thunderbird on the wild drive to the Island and swears if she will calm down, he will bring her a present every year from the Island, and he repeats his long–range plan for being her second husband. By present, he means a gift of something like a baby rabbit or a hawk feather. Poplar trees were just about to bloom then because the rain and sun had come just right on the trees, he explained. He found a snapping turtle, killed him with a stick, and said he would make her some soup which was known for its salubrious properties. A bowl of snapping turtle soup would fix anything that was wrong. He knows the kind of gift Laura will accept; he knows other gifts are wasted efforts.

In the middle of the river on the old bridge foundation, in July, it happened: The sex that may have made Anne Moorefield Hill, notwithstanding the sex, of course, with Jeremy. Laura loved Jeremy.

In her dreams, Laura may think she can change the facts, the smaller ones anyway: Laura pulling Henry down into the river, pulling off her shirt and jeans, believing in her wedding, thinking about Jeremy who can stand in the path of a train, wondering, testing him with this night with Henry. It may have taken Henry a while, maybe twenty minutes, to walk into the river, to come up to her as she stood there in the current shirtless, jeans-less. Not knowing what meant what, how he was being used—and if he had known, he would have been glad, would have been available. Take me, take me. Drink me, Drink me.

She swam underwater, drifted downstream away from him, kicked up a storm of water at him as she floated away, kicking more then less. At first, he had turned his back on her and yelled at her over his shoulder. He kept talking in all his ways of talking—white college boy, rap, what he called Old and Middle English mixed with early rapper, street dude, drug king, mall prowler, pimp, and a new language he says made up in cyberville on the net.

"Go on, girl. What you doing out there without your clothes. Something bad might happen to you soon, real soon if someone besides me who's got his eyes closed real tight saw you acting like you lost your mind. Get out the river this minute and get back up here on this fallen down bridge, put your clothes back on, or let's go, you and I, sit us down on that sandbank where the Indians used to bury dead Indians sitting up. That will be real interesting, a field trip, and will take your mind off the evil that it looks like to me is definitely on your mind, what is left of it. Come on, talk some of that trash you talk so good, some of that college trash, so I can get ready to finish college and get ready, get some money made, get jacked to be your second husband. I want to graduate and make a pile of money and wait for you and Jeremy to do your thing, have your two little babies, remember Anne and Emma, or you could call them Catherine and Elinor, that's all that's in this young man's mind waiting on the riverbank for you tonight."

Then desperate, Henry had called to her, "Watch out, there's a water moccasin swimming beside your leg."

Throwing her head back, laughing at him, shaking her hair and standing up in the waist deep water, running so clear she could see her feet on the sandy bottom in the moonlight, see the fish swimming around her legs, nibbling as they passed.

July. Two hundred years ago, two months almost before the wedding. The test, the second train test for Jeremy and Henry.

Henry yells at Laura. "Get out of that river, go find Jeremy Hill to get off with. My best friend, remember, your husband to be. Get drunk if it's too hard to take, but compose yourself, stop this liquefaction of your clothes, and in short, act right. All that college stuff we learned about the sexual revolution, hitching up and switch–hitting has turned you around. Done something ugly to you."

Henry tries to laugh. "Old Jeremy won't like it when I tell him how you have been acting, skinny dipping with your bare ass, excuse me, and bare breasts in my face. Don't you expose your sweet self to me. I am only human, well maybe I am not. Maybe this is a dream. Anyway, I got me girls, ones who know when and where to take off their clothes, girls with sense and manners. Ones who can keep me occupied until you have finished the first act with my friend Jeremy Hill. Those girls don't act like this. I do hate to say it, my sweet darling, but this is truly trashified behavior. Polluting the river on a nice summer night. And me, a handicapped candidate, a brachially–challenged one.

"Megan, for instance, respects me and will not, *would not* compromise me, take advantage of the way I am. And she wants in the worst way for me to be her first and last husband, though she understands the pre–nup I would draw up, apprizing her of my intentions to… well, you know the rest."

Henry jumps in the river with his clothes on, wrestles Laura down under the water, holding her head under until she thinks she has gone too far this time.

As she sleeps, Laura relaxes enough to think about Henry in the way he would have liked her to—holding her under water, but not, never intending to drown her: a second husband, long–suffering and passion spent, posting to her bidding, he would describe it. She had to go and ruin, he said later, that ideal he had of himself. She turned him, that night in July, into a kind of movie Indian, riding bareback, leaning down at just the right minute to pick a wild flower and then galloping across a river to bring it to her. Rescuing her after she almost drowned. If he had held her a few seconds longer, in fact, she would have drowned, be dead, buried, and out of this trouble.

In her dreams, Laura and Henry can be themselves, but in daylight he is what he is, the best friend, the father, he hopes of unborn Anne, but not the husband of Anne's mother. In July, they had talked about why he loved her, why, why, and why she was choosing to hit on him before they were ready for it. Was it what the brothers called a mercy fuck? Did she want to shatter his love for her, so she could get on with her life, her wedding?

When she explained in shouts from the river that she had devised a test for Jeremy—did he really love her enough to allow her to have sex, to put it simply, this night in July with Henry? That was the test, and it was not only a test for Jeremy—she wanted to show Rebecca and Weldon something about love, about being married, an arrangement that should take and withstand anything fate could dish out or think up. And she had thought of this: have sex with Henry before she married Jeremy. Pregnancy, Anne, that was a terrible, old–fashioned surprise, though it is not exactly what has driven Jeremy away. It is the Henry element. Then Henry, in her dream, hands Laura a wild rhododendron branch, shocked into silence at her cold–blooded/hot–blooded plan. Then he runs toward her plunging in the river.

She comes up for air, she is clawing at his wet jeans, holding onto his belt ripping the neck of his tee shirt and crying with the little air she could get.

Time and events, the river, the sex, the pregnancy melt into one picture of the river last July. In Laura's dreams, maybe Henry talks his Green Knight talk, his English and psych–major talk.

Asleep, Laura can make sense of her life. Henry can bring her ice rattled out of the thermos he brought for them with his mother's biscuits. They lie on the hot concrete pilings in the middle of the river.

It's a July night, the eighth. Things were simple; things were possible. She explained to him what women want because he was so sure he knew what women want—him. He rolled off the concrete slab laughing down into the river. His ankles were crossed, head resting on a rock that jutted up out of the shallow water making a little white froth so he could breathe. Pleased with himself, he can't hear what she is saying. She gets angry. He stays down so long she grabs his foot and he lunges straight up and pulls her down to lie on the river bed with him. They kiss in the white water that runs around their heads on the rock.

Laura settles down into straight narratives, the secret stories she replays in her sleep, called "How Laura and Jeremy Fell Apart" and "How Laura and Henry Almost Got Together." She cannot wake up until she makes sense of the two stories.

It does not dawn on her that she must explain to Rebecca and Weldon all of these things. For once, she does not know how to begin.

Chapter Nine

Rebecca and Weldon are leaving home together for the first time since the wedding—three months of house arrest. They are taking Gram, all bundled up for the December rain. She has not been out in the car for longer than that, at least six months.

They have lost their minds. "What little I have left anyway," says Gram as she holds her arms toward Weldon for his help. Rebecca says no, she is the one who has lost hers completely.

Henry will drive.

"Don't leave me out of the mindless population." Weldon is wheeling Gram out to the car, lifting her out into the front seat of Henry's Thunderbird, folding up the wheel chair and putting it in the trunk. "Mine's gone, lost too."

Leaving Laura at home, they will shock her back into her life. They will wake her up. It's a simple idea (surprisingly simple since it's Henry's) but they are "executing it." They are afraid that if they do not act now—Laura is six months pregnant—that they will kill the baby cocooned in Laura, who will die, is dying, of unhappiness. They will kill two people if they keep on making milkshakes and telling stories and failing to get the doctors to admit Laura to the hospital.

Any idea is better than none, any change, it can't be too simple. They must not rush home and find everything exactly the same as when they left: Laura ruined, hating her life, unable, unwilling to take the five steps—Henry has stepped them off—across the floor from her bed to Anne's crib set up there by Henry (his old crib from home) to wait for Anne's birth. "A detail," he says, in the long scheme of things.

Anne is with him already, and he hopes, prays, and begs fate that she will be with Laura in a new way at the end of the evening, with her mother, part of Laura in a new way. Accepted. Acknowledged. All that good stuff.

Will Laura hear Anne's cries when and if she is born? Will Laura know what her cries mean? Will she care? She has never heard a baby's cries, never babysat when she was a girl. She did not have a normal home; she would not do normal girl things.

Rebecca and Gram feel foolish and helpless, unwomanly, and unnatural, reduced to trying such a terrible and stupid thing—go out to dinner, deserting Laura, five months pregnant who has been in bed since she came home from her wedding.

It's not possible, is it, to force Laura to want her baby? Weldon says anything is possible. They must think along those lines of possibilities. He's stopped drinking... think about it!

But girls do kill unborn babies and themselves. Or after the babies are born. Women starve and beat their children to death. Many young women kill themselves in many ways. These thoughts occur among the thoughts about what is possible.

They want, like earnest graduation speakers, to force Laura to feel her life's worth, its value, and to feel her baby's life and all that it means. Henry says that the space that they are providing when they leave her, the Pascalian spaces, will or may jolt her. Absence can and does make a fonder, and a stronger heart. It's worth a try. "Give it a whirl," he says, grim as death. Absence can stimulate: it can splash down over the psyche, cold water in a water fall, arousing with its cruel startle, it can kiss the sleeping beauty. Better than the one–armed prince has for sure.

An item in the newspaper last week has made them feel more desperate, more uncertain of what to do and more anxious to try anything, no matter how stupid or silly. A deer hunter had led a state trooper to the remains of an unidentified body just off the interstate approximately two and a half miles from the Waynesboro exit. Deer do come close to populated areas and the sheriff says it was not unusual for deer to turn toward the interstate. "It was that early snow fall, in early December, that evidently drove the deer toward the interstate. Without that snow, we would not have discovered the body," the trooper said to reporters. The body was discovered in a ravine. The packs of wild dogs in the area made identification difficult, and there were no items of clothing and no personal effects. The forensics lab will make every effort to resolve the situation. Officials have not positively identified the individual; however, Trooper Martin speculated that it may have been a young man trying to get to the interstate to hitchhike. Disorientation often occurs in hikers who underestimate distances and leave their camping sites without food or water and carry no identification. The investigation will continue. Trooper Martin says that foul play is not indicated. No signs of weapons used or of a struggle; it was more a case of exposure and homelessness. The individual could be from anywhere, being this close to the interstate. The problem of dumping bodies is increasing. Cases are kept open for years as they hope for a break. The computer search has identified two victims in its five years of operation. That's a pretty good record for found remains.

Rebecca and Weldon do not understand anything about the lives they are living, though they have perfected the routines of observing, entertaining and nursing Laura, if those are the words for their new lives of talking to the doctors and cooking things they think will make Laura stronger in only a few swallows. Getting through the days toward January which would be a seven month pregnancy is what they have set as their ideal. Forget March and nine months.

Henry is now an expert at how little time a baby needs in her mother's uterus to survive. He knows the case of a sixteen week old fetus who is now eight years old and plays soccer and chess. Every day gotten through with Laura is cause for celebration for Henry. This trip away from her for three hours will tear him apart, limb—of the three left, he says—from limb. And so, driving in the cold rain of late December is what they are doing tonight, driving over a fault in the surface of their lives.

Henry has read about this shock treatment, as he calls it. He says it verges on sadism, but so what if it works. They are doing the worst thing: abandoning an (unborn) baby to the dangers of being with her very ill mother, and all, *all* in the name of saving them both. Drive your addicted, for instance, children out into the storm, for example, so they know they must change if they want to survive the blizzard. The wind cuts their faces and they taste blood. They return to the door, wipe their feet, and come in to do homework, do some chores, find their place in the family birth order or world order. Prodigal children cast out can return cured of their attitudes, their mental illness.

The fatted calf slaughtered for the feast of celebration is appropriate. It's a ridiculous perversion of the bible story what they are doing, but they go forward under Henry's orders not knowing what else to do.

That's the theory Henry says, locking kids out of the home to force them to see that they need their home, but their case is different, and they must make adjustments for it, translate the treatment to suit the exigencies of their situation. The danger to Laura and unborn–but–still–alive Anne is to continue in the same way: sleeping, sleeping, not exercising, not eating, not thinking, not planning, not explaining, not, not, nothing, nada. Too much home, in a word.

Of course, in their absence, Laura could panic and wander out of the house in a daze, in a fog of misery, and that would be, could be worse. If she should feel alone and panic and what...

Are they going that far? Harrying Laura out of the house in the December rains to die of exposure as the hiker who was or may have been Jeremy Hill? They do not know if or how long she can stand up! She has gained five pounds, a poor record even for babies in the Third World, the doctor said when they went in last time. Would Laura leave the house when their absence made itself known, would she stand by the side of the road or lie down in a ditch to die? Would someone come along and put her in his car or white pickup? And then what? Is Jeremy Hill out there living in the woods, watching them not save Laura, watching them abandon her? Or is Jeremy Hill dead, the unidentified body ravaged by the wild dogs in the ravine near Waynesboro?

Jeremy's parents do not call any more. The last time they called they said they would not call again until, unless they had some news. Rebecca did not tell them about Jeremy's visit. How would she have told them about that day when he appeared in the kitchen with the knife? Your son, feared dead, is a killer at heart? Your son.

Hospitals won't keep Laura—they have tried the ones in Richmond and Charlottesville. An institution that looks like a college campus except for fences and locked gates, that's what they need. They feel sure that Laura would like to be left to die, and a ditch would suit her fine. She does not want to live. That's the problem. Henry has never read in all of his books of a case quite like Laura's. Pre-partum depressions last maybe six months, and they are up to five. It was September, three hundred years ago, when she walked home from the mountains looking by the time she got home as if she had been mauled by a mountain wild cat.

Henry thinks there is one chance, one in a million, if they all—Weldon, even Gram, Rebecca, himself—are not at home to do everything for Laura for a few hours—that Laura may get up and walk across her room, look at her baby's crib, at least look down where her beautiful baby Anne will sleep, Baby Anne who must anticipate from the womb, he says, her mother's eyes resting on her face coming to rest on the tiny face as if they belonged there. Baby Anne will hear her mother's voice directed at her the way mothers talk to their babies, the way Rebecca (Henry has been calling them Rebecca and Weldon) talked to Laura when she was a baby. The way Vivian talked to him as a baby, if he ever were one, he says, the way she probably would like to talk to him still. The way Jeremy Hill's mother talked to him—though possibly she did not and that is one source of the problem they are all trapped in now.

Henry thinks that this microcosmic, staged, artificial evening which he calls "Away from Laura", this reprieve from their ordinary lives, might, just might, force Laura into realizing that everything, the future, rests on her, that she is *it*, she is carrying the ball, it is her hand on the trigger, she is the one who knows the code, she has her finger in the dyke, she— If Laura can feel that moment register deeply and fully in isolation, it may drive the nail or hypodermic into her heart and make her want to live. One tincture, one breath of, call it freedom, yes, freedom from their hovering over and around her, may drive reality into Laura's brain. The nail of freedom.

They are reduced to these bitter simplicities, Henry says. Icons, he smiles, across the tool bar of possibilities—nail, needle, ball, trigger. Laura may feel free to be her old self, wake up and start explaining things again. She may stare at the crib or out the window, at the phone, even at the refrigerator, or out the door, or...

If she does not make any move toward ordinary life, they do not know what they will do next. Weldon says that they will move to Hawaii or Alaska or to what used to be Yugoslavia, to ruined Sarajevo. Hawaii, the waves. Alaska, the snow. What used to be Saigon? But tonight, everything hangs on her being alone for the first time since she came home from her wedding trip. Jeremy Hill may be alive, out there somewhere. Maybe he is not the dead hiker. DNA tests take longer in Richmond than they do on television shows. He may come back as he swore he would last month. There have not been any more signs of his having stood at a window as he must have in the first three weeks in October, no more footprints. He may be a smear of bones on a slide in the lab.

And what if they kill the baby by causing a deeper trauma, leaving Laura, who is, it is clear to them, an ill and dangerous person though Henry will not let them say such a thing. He points out that denial is a better state to be in than many other states. People used to say a person had a nervous breakdown. Of course, that is what is happening, Laura is having one. They used to think mentally ill people were a threat, and it is true that they are contagious. So they do not mean the harm they do. So?

Henry insists that they stay the course, that this one evening out on an old–fashioned date, is what they need to try, a *reductio ad absurdum*, maybe, but also maybe a hammering to an airy thinness of the problem, and he adds, besides, all may yet be well.

The leaving–Laura idea is one of many he says he wants them to try. Gram says why not. They have tried many other things, including mild doses of serotonin–elevators from the doctors, everything else. Weldon has agreed to it. Go to the Rivanna Restaurant! Here they will take their stand and let their absence create freedom, albeit an artificial kind, for Laura to take control of her life to become, and here Henry says there is a wealth of possible expressions, self–directed, autonomous, ready to live.

No one at home with Laura: that is the first rule, and the second is no one can leave the table at the restaurant—these are the uncomplicated rules. They will be chained to the booth by the hope that they are shocking Laura back to life. They will guard each other against breaking loose to rush (Gram, of course, cannot rush, but she could go call the sheriff, whose mother she taught). Henry would... what? Tackle Weldon to the floor? Cause a scene on the brick linoleum of the Rivanna Restaurant? A one–armed man, Henry says, can be fatal. He looks at Weldon and Rebecca. Gram pats his arm.

Henry says Laura's depression is anger that has frozen into silence and withdrawal, and he adds that he may be wrong to think they can break up the ice in Laura, thaw it to get her started back toward life.

The facts of their lives are stunning. They do not need Henry to tell them this, but for some reason, they like for him to remind them over and over: they have a daughter whose husband blew up the car on the honeymoon (or a daughter who rammed the honeymoon car into a tree and blew it up—either way, one of the couple lost his or her mind on their camping trip), they have a granddaughter on the way, they have a daughter who refuses to live in any real sense of the word, a daughter who will not wake up long enough to be pregnant reasonably. They have a son–in–law who may be dead. And, plus or minus, pro or con, they have a marriage that is no longer broken.

At the restaurant, Weldon will talk about moving them all to Fairbanks if the plan they are in the middle of does not work, if they hear the rescue squad or the fire truck go past the restaurant in the direction, twenty–four miles away, of their house where Laura is sleeping or waking when kissed by their absence.

Here in the red booth, Weldon can force himself to talk of returning to farming: strip farming, rotation of small grain, corn and hay, water sheds, and the 115 bushels of corn per acre he might get next year from Elk Island if he found the right man to farm it. It's crazy, but it is talk that makes its own kind of sense. Internally consistent, Henry says, talking about helping in any way he can.

They will listen gladly, grateful for Henry's latest remedy

for Laura who is slipping into deeper and longer periods of sleeping. She does not seem to know that her parents have the marriage she always wanted them to have, now over her almost–dead body.

Many times since the wedding they have rushed her back to the hospital, hoping that the doctors would keep her, but they won't, even when she seemed to have stopped breathing, the emergency room monitor beeping like the birds caught in their chimneys. New insurance regulations, new hospital policies, no coverage for a problem with depression, and even when Rebecca tells the admission clerk that those considerations are beside the point— Weldon does not have benefits; Rebecca does not—the doctors will not keep Laura at the hospital.

They all hope that underneath her sleep, Laura is listening to every word Weldon has said about their new lives—her parents' marriage, the plans to work in Sarajevo or Fairbanks or Saigon—and that she is trying not to fall further away from them. She stirs when Weldon comes in the house, when his boots scrape on the porch, that is, she turns over and seems to bury deeper under the quilts Gram made her. They sit in her room and talk for hours: another one of Henry's ideas.

They have waited for some sign of a change, they have gone to the outer limits of themselves, of hope, of patience, hoping that she will sit up slowly, ask for some juice or toast, then settle back and ask a question. A sign is all they want, not recovery, not yet. They are not greedy.

Henry says after tonight if they fail to accomplish their mission—his words—they will take Laura to a hospital out of state, he will continue his computer search until he finds one that will keep her until Anne is born. But he wants to try this one thing before they turn themselves over to the authorities—his phrase again.

Henry sleeps on the floor in Laura's room. He calls their house the "Cauthorn Convalescent Villa."

His plan is so simple it may work. While they are at the restaurant, Laura will wake up, see that they are all gone, even Gram, even Henry. This is the theory, their fervent theory–prayer, simple–minded, idiotic. They have neighbors—the O'Brians, the Thompkins, the Walkers—who have known them, known Gram's family, Rebecca's parents, have known Weldon's family—the Nelsons and the Cauthorns forever, but Rebecca and Weldon feel as if they have just moved to Rivanna, as if they were some of the new people who have bought up slots of land to the river where they are building log cabins and vacation homes from kits as if there would never be a flood, people from Baltimore and Norfolk who think they are getting back to basics out here.

It is worse now for Weldon and Rebecca than it was after Kelly Brightley and Dennis Johnson were killed. Much worse. Illness is much worse, socially, than fatal accidents. People are bored with the vagueness of illness, the lack of detail, the sameness. And cancer or emphysema is easier, socially, than depression. People answer their own questions. "Laura's about the same?" they ask and answer. Their eyes fasten on Rebecca's forehead or her shoulders. They are uncomfortable. The name Jeremy Hill does not come up. They would say that they never really knew him. He does not occur to them. The wedding is disconnected from the social life of Rivanna like a lamp or phone. It did not mean anything.

Henry thinks there is one chance in a thousand that

his plan will work. They will get out of the house and put the plan of desertion into action. Gram and Rebecca will sit in the back seat, Henry will drive with Weldon riding shotgun. They feel that they are planning a bank robbery. They have never talked about leaving Laura before, but it seemed obvious and inevitable when Henry announced what they would do. Last ditch, amateur effort before going professional when they call in the heavies and commit her to a psychiatric hospital, a Westbrook or Tucker's Pavilion, private pay, twenty–four hour suicide watch, restraints, monitored drug therapies. For this option, they will need a psychiatric evaluation and Jeremy Hill's signature. Or move away, all of them, to a place near the hospital that Henry finds with his computer.

Last week Weldon was showing Henry how he fed a hawk. Henry had said hawks cannot be tamed or taught to come to feeders. The art of falconry is not feeding the birds—he had read a book about it. Then he saw Weldon's hawk light and eat the pieces of raw chicken Weldon was putting out on the big rock in the back yard. That's when Henry knew, he says, that they should try anything.

The mistletoe clump high in the oak was as big as a man's head, and has some ice on it, the first of the year. Seeing it when the hawk flew up from his chicken tenders, his McNuggets, "determined their course" Henry said.

"The impossible is all around us waiting for an opportunity to go into action. The hawk came down to feed! Sweet!"

They should go out, Henry said. He stood there looking up at the dripping mistletoe shaking from the hawk's weight on the branch. They agreed as if the hawk and the mistletoe were signals to them. Plus, they have no other choices at this point because the hospitals near them do not want Laura.

"Try TLC, try stimulation, try your own home remedies—nothing by mouth or vein—just social and emotional stimulants," the doctors have said, this last time with tired exasperation.

Rebecca puts on her brown suit with the gold thread in the material, a far cry, as Henry would have said if he had known the story (and maybe he does, who knows) of the green–gold dress that night on Elk Island with Weldon, and then she helped Gram into her blue wool. They are ready for an evening at the Rivanna Restaurant.

They swear to themselves to stay at least three hours if it kills them. Henry synchronizes their watches. They will not leave to come home until ten–thirty. Weldon is looking at the gibbous moon.

It is possible for a baby to die *in utero* from emotional neglect. It is possible to die of heartbreak, of sadness. The house could burn, not the rocks but all the wood in it, down to the ground. Houses do burn all the time, killing the abandoned children, burnt alive, left at home by parents who dressed up to go out and then went, exactly as they are doing.

Weldon fills the wood stove with oak wood so it would burn slowly, and the little stove in Laura's room. The dampers are almost completely closed, but sometimes the wind can get caught in the chimney and blow back down, back through the stove, forcing black smoke of the front of the stove. Smoke kills before fire.

Laura's husband has disappeared and her friend who may be the father of her baby is living with them. That's it in a nutshell. No one but Henry and Laura know that the paternity is not a sure thing. Surely Jeremy Hill is the father of the unborn baby, and he is missing. They do not know who Anne's biological father is yet. It seems unimportant, and Henry says *he* is the father, regardless of tests. *De facto. In loco*, he calls himself, or loco. But Jeremy is the father on paper, though what paper?

Weldon and Rebecca used to have part–time jobs with a few benefits. Now, neither one goes to work. Gram will be eighty–six in July. Rebecca has to keep tabs on what their lives are.

They are a shock to everyone at the restaurant. First because they are there at all, second because they have left Laura at home, not that it is commented on. Everyone expects Laura to kill herself. They don't know she is pregnant, though they may suspect it. But the thought of suicide is obvious, written all over people. They know what people are thinking, people know somehow what is going on with them at home. When they walk into the Rivanna, wheeling Gram in her chair, they go down the row of booths heading for the one the farthest from the door. It is five minutes after eight.

A husband is far down the list of what they want for Laura. They have Henry. They want basics—instincts—to take over, the big things—hunger, muscles twitching to move, to hold, to nurse, to lift a small warm thing. Then they can worry about paternity, husbands, farms, Gram's tachycardia, money for inoculation, college. Little things.

Henry talks to Laura and walks miles in her room, as if he were holding the baby, miming holding the future baby with his left arm, feeding the imagined Anne and walking her, singing to her and reading to her. But there is a furiousness to it all. Of course, there is.

The doctors almost shrugged when they sent them home after the last visit to the hospital. "Home cures," they said, busy with their live–baby and neo–natal work, not expecting Henry to take it literally, not knowing that Laura never even sits up except when they sit her up, then she stays there until she slumps down again, sleeping. She goes into her bathroom and runs the water briefly. They hear the flushing toilet which cheers them. Signs of life.

The ringing phone—they all lean toward the restaurant's kitchen where the one phone hangs on the wall. Gram and Rebecca are afraid of the telephone—it's not quite the cell phone era yet in Rivanna—and they expect to be told that the sheriff has found a *situation* at their house. Gram and Rebecca hope, they pray, that Laura is calling to ask them to come home. Did she hear them say where they were going, will she see the phone number of the restaurant pinned to her counterpane? She needs them to rush home immediately because the house is burning down and she has wrapped herself up in a blanket and has driven to Henry's shack, the one on the Island where he goes when he slips out of the house for an hour at the longest. She has called them on the portable phone. They must leave for home immediately, their burning home.

They jackknife over the booth table, half–up out of their seats. Then they sink back and hope with all their hearts for a small catastrophe, anything to wake Laura up, to snag her attention. But they know that Laura is too ill to get up and drive to Henry's shack, to use his car phone, even use the one by her bed. They must not go home. Yet.

Marie Marshall who owns the restaurant is still on the phone in the kitchen, but they cannot hear what she is saying. At last, she comes to their table.

"Come back next week so you can talk to my children, not Megan, the older children, so I won't have to." Marie laughs. "You don't know them as well as you know Megan, in fact, not at all. They quiz me to see if I am having any dates yet, but I don't think it's any of their business, do you? You may not know that George and I have separated, last month, that I am getting the restaurant in the settlement. You don't know either that Megan will be helping me—doing the books, not the dishes. For this, she has a hundred thousand dollar liberal arts education, the one she got with Laura, and you probably know that she is expecting a baby in late April."

This is the first conversation Rebecca and Weldon have had with anyone outside their foursome (they don't count Laura) since the wedding or the visits with the Moorefields the day after. They try to make sense out of what Marie is saying. It is too angular and complicated in a normal way. Marie and George's other children—a banker and an interior designer—they hardly know, Marie is right. Megan is pregnant as Henry reported. They don't feel that they can ask anything. They nod and smile.

Marie is going on about how she wants to be able to say to these older accomplished children, "See, I have friends. A life. Some people enjoy my company, they come to my restaurant."

Marie doesn't seem worried about Megan, who is taking classes on single parenting and Lamaze—in that order, she laughs.

Marie's two older children want their mother to be married, and now they probably want to know who Megan has been "dating" and want her married too. They support Marie in her separation from their dad, but they do not want her to date anyone who might need nursing, or who is in financial trouble—they say *financial shit*, according to Marie—or someone who is a control freak. They have this person, this stranger, this never–never man, all picked out for her.

Marie does not want to marry anyone. Been there, done that, she says. Marie does not say what Megan would like. That does not seem to be an issue, and evidently, Megan's loving Henry is history. These problems seem remote, simple, enviable.

Rebecca and Weldon, Marie is glad to see, have "worked it out" and are back together. What is their secret she wants to know. She and George after all those years, three kids, everything, just gave up. She does not know until they tell her that Laura is pregnant, but she has heard that she is at home and is ill.

Rebecca and Weldon do, in fact, feel deeply married on one point: they want Laura to get up out of her bed and walk across the room. Henry is also married to them on that point, and to Gram. This marriage of the four of them is as strong as a cathedral.

Rebecca and Weldon recall the summer evenings out on Marie and George's dock, down from the cottage, the one they bought from Evelyn and Tatie Byrd. The rock patio. The snapping turtles floating with their heads just breaking the surface of the lake seem a thousand years ago when Megan and Laura were very young, and the Marshalls' older children were away at camps. These evenings get mixed in with those evenings with Tatie and Evelyn Byrd reciting poetry there before the Marie and George moved to Rivanna. In an artificial voice, Rebecca tries to tell Henry about it. Remembered good times.

The thought of children frightens them. Jeremy Hill

is dead—it comes to them—he must be the hiker in the newspaper. Laura acts as if she is dead. She and Megan, her childhood friend, are pregnant.

They have gone out for supper at the Rivanna Restaurant whose "All Night" swirls in old fashioned green tubes that collectors now want to go with their old coke signs and bottles, Marie tells them.

"What can I get you?" Marie asks them under the ropes of running cedar still up from Christmas. Her pearls with the diamond and sapphire clasp swing near their faces over her L.L. Bean wrap around apron. Is she overdressed to work in the restaurant? She comes back to them, leaving the telephone hanging, swinging a little the kitchen wall. Marie has a glass in each hand, two wines, two beers coming. They had not asked for anything. She gives people what she thinks they need.

She ducks under a pine bough tied to the exposed beam of the ceiling. They copy her, stooping from their sitting positions, when she walks under the cedar ropes, tilting their heads slightly. There is some drying mistletoe tied at eye–level too, staring at them.

"Now, what for supper, good people?" Marie laughs at them for their sympathetic nodding. Weldon asks who is on the phone still hanging down. They do not explain that they are expecting a call from a person who is not able to call herself, to walk to the phone in the kitchen or even stretch out her hand to the one on her bedside table. Laura may be in such straits that someone else has read the note pinned to her counterpane and is calling them to come home. The sheriff or the volunteer firemen may want to talk to the next of kin.

Who says older women can't be sexy? Marie has on leather pants, silk blouse, gold bracelet, shining hose and her Christmas apron. Laura could grow old, have difficult children who have opinions about her dating and the way she dresses. She could have a life like Marie's.

Why can't old people have the babies? Weldon and Rebecca would know how to pick up a baby, their Anne, feed her, change her, everything. They would dress in soft colors and take Anne out for rides and views of the river. They would go on educational trips with big scooped–out safety engineered car seats strapped in the back. Rebecca and Weldon, with Henry taking over, would know how to heat bottles. Henry says men have the capacity to lactate, he's read about it in the *New England Journal of Medicine*. Gram knows how to make a baby happy enough to sleep all night. Rebecca and Weldon will stay married forever. Gram will do what she has to do and die quietly when she has seen Anne through her babyhood.

Women like Marie know how to walk, how to lean over men especially ones with dead wives or who have had chemo themselves and appreciate swinging pearls and flashing ankles. Tonight the men in the restaurant wear plaid vests and bow ties, hand–tied. They voted against raising taxes, but not, they say, because they didn't want better schools.

Weldon and Rebecca drink in this talk. Marie wants her restaurant to make a go of it so her older children will give her a break. Rebecca and Weldon really must come more often. And Mrs. Cauthorn and Henry too, Laura and Megan's friend. She does not seem to remember that Megan, her perfect daughter, loved Henry, that someone might think that Megan is pregnant with Henry's child. No one there in the restaurant thinks that, and those who know the principals, that is the four of them, the double

dating four—Gram and Henry, Weldon and Rebecca—
know that it is outrageous to think that Henry is the father
of another baby. If he is the father of any baby, it's Laura's.
They feel defensive and angry about this paternity issue,
and absurd.

They cannot sit still any longer, cannot stand it. Now,
Marie has hung up the phone. She never said who was
calling and waiting as it was swinging. Surely the state
police were not waiting while the phone was swinging.
Surely, the doctor in Richmond had another emergency to
deal with. The fire department got another call. Rebecca
and Weldon know they are not making sense even to
themselves about this phone thing.

They begin trying to get up from the booth. They
enjoyed their dinners, what Marie chose for them—the
veal, the medallions, the winter squash, very, very good.
Gram promises to return, and then adds brilliantly, bravely,
heroically, "We'll bring Laura."

As if, as if. And maybe they have jolted Laura out of her
death bed by now.

It is nine forty–five.

Like them, maybe Marie wishes everything were
different, that she were anywhere else. Rebecca and Weldon
are ashamed of their lives, of not knowing what to do next,
desperate for new stratagems for reviving Laura: the crib,
the mobiles, the toys for the baby, things a baby can't begin
to deal with for years, the tricycle, the computer.

They hear Marie laughing, Maria who used to ruin her
own parties by apologizing too many times for the cottage,
but at the restaurant, she doesn't apologize. She has
changed. She is now a movie star kind of person. She may
go on dates. She has employed her unmarried pregnant

daughter in her restaurant and divorced her husband of thirty–one years.

What should they call Jeremy Hill now? Henry's best friend? A suicide, Laura's husband, Anne's father? What do they call Henry? Laura's friend, Laura's next husband, Anne's father/stepfather, their tenant on the Island?

The phone rings again. This time Rebecca walks toward its ringing knowing it is for them. They should not be at a restaurant, they should not have come. They know that. They will be in jail for criminal negligence tonight or next week. The ringing tells them that again. It is not possible to help Laura by being absent. The old way is best: presence, staying, lingering, getting in the way, driving crazy, lurking, being there on guard, at the post. All those years of staying away, leaving. Laura was right in essence, in brief, *in toto*.

"Tell Laura hello. I'd really like to get together, have her come to the cottage." Marie says to Gram as she takes away their dishes to the kitchen toward the phone which Rebecca has almost reached, swimming through the thirteen foot waves.

Alma and Hill Brightley are walking in. Hill looks like an alcoholic not quite in recovery. He tilts his head to remove his hat but it seems to be a greeting to Weldon, so they take it that way and before they mean it or know what they mean, the Brightleys are moving toward the table they have been trying to leave.

Hill's blazer is double-breasted, his overcoat is black and rides on his shoulders. He has a wine glass in his hand, and Alma, like Marie, is overdressed. She has on a green velvet cape, of all things, with a hood. They look as if they were just leaving an opera or the circus.

They are smiling. He turns in a slow spin, trying to head, maybe, Alma away from the Cauthorn table, but he says in passing to Weldon that he's been drinking all afternoon, telling the truth the way few drinkers do. Alma turns toward the door, but to close it behind them, not to leave, not to avoid the Cauthorns. With the door open, the wet December air blows in. The phone has stopped after only four rings.

"We are having car trouble" Alma says. "It's running, that's the trouble, we can't cut it off." They laugh and say, "Listen." They hear it whining, and Henry says maybe it's the wiring.

They have stopped in to use the phone on the way home from Richmond. They are glad to see Rebecca and Weldon because they have wanted to tell them that they did enjoy coming to Laura's wedding, and they know that Laura must have felt awkward or unsure about inviting them after all the time that has passed and after what happened to Kelly, but they have wanted Laura to know that it was a wonderful help to them to be there and to think of Kelly as older, as Laura's age. They felt—hard to believe it themselves—free for that stretch of time at the wedding, free from the sad memories of Kelly, the ones that had congealed around her at fourteen when she and Dennis had the accident. Laura probably has no idea what her wedding meant to them. And they hope that in some way they are related to the Hill family, and that Hill who got his name, he has no idea how, is a long lost cousin to Laura's young man. They sit down. Marie comes over with two cups of coffee, and says she is bringing four more, or three with one tea for Gram.

Weldon and Rebecca feel strokes approaching, cancer

metastasizing. Marie calls someone to help the Brightleys with their car. Marie knows the number of the mechanic; Marie knows everything. She takes Hill's coat and walks it back to the row of pegs to put with the other coats.

Marie can do anything. She is a datable, divorced woman. Again, it's time for them all to leave, after an eternity.

It's ten twenty–three.

Hill Brightley turns to Weldon and says "One more thing that we have thought of since the wedding. We were wrong to ask you to write that letter, and we want you to know how sorry we are. The invitation to the wedding made us see things clearly. First time in a long time." Then he compliments Marie on the selections on her menu.

"Catfish Cajun style! Hot chafing dishes of rosemaried carrots! Who would believe it. In Rivanna!" Alma is saying she is so glad she came because she almost did not. Mozart is Hill's thing, not hers, and they have just been to Richmond to a high school production of *The Magic Flute*. Terrible. But she wants to say the same thing to them about the letter. She manages her coffee, sweeping off the hood of the beautiful cape.

"Are you wondering where this came from?"

Henry says his mother has one from Ireland, he thinks, and it is an opera cape, isn't it?

"Ridiculous, isn't it? But I thought I should wear it if I wanted to." Alma laughs, lightly as the sugar she sifts into her coffee. She has heard, she stirs, she sips, fairy-godmotherly, that Laura is at home, and she would like to come to see her.

She finishes her coffee and is helping the Cauthorns leave—the wheelchair awkwardness, the coats.

Marie tries to get them all to stay, she wants them to try her new pie, not, she promises, the same old key limes, but a sweet potato–pineapple–pecan dream chiffon. She wants them to talk about the closed landfills, the suicide of the dentist who stepped out of his office into the path of the truck, the calves trapped in the sudden ice on the ponds last week, she wants to tell them how George is making it as a bachelor and how they are in some ways closer than they ever were married. She reminds them about Laura and Megan being together in their pregnancies. They are watching the swing of her pearls.

Alma Brightley is happy to know that Laura is pregnant. And Marie wants Alma to know that Megan is.

"Laura is ill," Rebecca says to Alma. "Please do come to see her soon. You will understand, I am sure, at least as much as we do, her illness."

"Depression?" Alma turns her spoon over. "We will come tomorrow morning, or tonight if you don't think it's too late—not just because we have always loved your Laura who invited us to her wedding after all the trouble and sadness. But, please excuse what sounds like a joke in this conversation—we can't turn our car off and so it suits us to come now. I would like to tell Laura about being depressed when I was expecting Kelly. I stayed in bed the whole nine months, gained eighty pounds, had edema, almost lost her, almost drove Hill away, tried to run away myself. And then, she was born. Of course, of course, there was the terrible accident, but Kelly was with us, coming at us with both guns blazing, Hill likes to say, for fourteen years—all wonderful ones. But, Laura may not understand this part, and I would love to talk to her. She was so kind, so kind to include us in her wedding when she knew how difficult it would be. Being there meant, well, everything to us, as I hope I have said. Because Kelly was not there, but others were there. I am talking too much as I do, and not making sense, so I will stop. Laura will not mind if she is like I was, having someone talk to her, talk at her, as she lies in the bed these last months. I know. I do know something about what she is going through, something, I think, though her situation is different from mine. You may not know that Hill had three children from an earlier marriage and his wife would not let him see the boys. After Kelly died, the boys came back to us, one by one. There are turns, in this life, I mean, that we do not and cannot expect. But I am going on again, I can see by the way Hill is looking at me. I guess we should go to Laura's now because the car is still running. Marie's mechanic can come to your house. We won't stay long. She won't mind, being depressed, that we came at an odd time or so late. Did I say that? I know a lot of little things about being depressed. I think that Laura will explain things when she knows that I know some of the things she does. Then, I feel almost certain, she will begin telling you. The car's running is a sign for us to go, don't you think?"

The fire is smoldering, Rebecca and Weldon hope, in the stoves at home. The two calls were not for the Cauthorns, but the telephone is ringing again as they leave with Alma and Hill Brightley following them in their car.

Henry will lead, driving his old Thunderbird in front of the Brightleys. Gram and Rebecca are wedged into the back seat and Weldon is up front with Henry. They are quiet and Henry drives as fast as he can to bring the Brightleys to Laura.

It's ten thirty–three by their watches.

CHAPTER TEN

Elizabeth James Hill was born on the sixth of March. Full term, after a four–hour Lamaze labor, in St. Mary's Hospital, five pounds two ounces, a little black topnotch of hair. Calm as a pearl. Nursed, slept. Slept and nursed.

Thirty–six hours later, they are back at home. Henry had read a book about Lamaze, read it out loud, practiced with Rebecca, and they did fine. Weldon said he would help if he could. He would do something, anything but that, Dear God, anything else. Not again. He had done it once. He meant it, and they could see that he did. He was doing many new things, and, as he said, had many new attitudes which surprised him daily.

When the nurse brought the birth certificate papers into Laura's room, Laura wrote Elizabeth James Hill. Henry did not say a word then about Anne, the "the putative baby Anne," he had called her.

"Forget Anne, long live Elizabeth. That's fine, very fine! Call her Ezekiel, call her Sam, Ishmael, feel free! I love, love, love her, and she's mine! By proclamation, degree, or gene, it makes no never mind to me, as long as she is here on earth, and not anywhere else, not with the blessing–showering Kelly."

He did not look disappointed not to have the name "Anne," though maybe surprised, when Laura wrote the name in the hospital register, explaining briefly: Elizabeth, for her first piano teacher who had put up with her; James, for the river, because they had all crossed a river and come to the other side; Hill, of course, for Jeremy. Then, the words came in a stream:

"I will always love Jeremy and take full responsibility for what happened. That is all I can do now. Acknowledge everything. Don't worry, I am not explaining what happened. I cannot. Maybe no one can."

These words sounded something like her old self, offering a small explanation or the semblance of one, a shadow of her former monologues.

Henry listens, grinning like crazy, adding, "Right, yes, me too, I agree. Word for word, Woman of Many Words, We Hope, Right on. You got that one right. Steady Eddy."

And so Laura is improving, gaining on herself. They can see it, every day. Alma Brightley is there, not as often as she had been in December. Many times she and Hill had spent the night in Laura's room, sitting up all night with her in the twin rocking chairs, Henry sleeping on his pallet on the floor. It was crowded in there. Crowded with love, Alma said, and Laura would feel it, certainly, and would not go join Kelly and Dennis, not yet, not yet, and all the clouds of witnesses of good things.

And so, when Elizabeth James Hill is seventeen days old, her mother marries Henry Moorefield, holding her in her arms. March the twenty-third, in the kitchen at home, the Stone House of Many Hopes, Henry now calls it.

It is a marriage in name only, to date, but all things come to him who waits, and Henry tells Laura that he is able and willing to wait through eternity or the day before. He is happy—even with their history of death and destruction because birth and marriage have followed. He says he is like the traditional bride, giddy, walking on air.

Rebecca made the cake Gram had always told them about, the pound cake made for wedding parties when she was a girl. She sat and helped Rebecca by saying "that's good, that's good," during the creaming of the pound of butter and pound of sugar, the adding of the twelve eggs one by one, and then the flour. Last, the grated lemon peel and drops of almond.

The day before, Weldon shot a wild turkey, even though the season had not opened; he skinned it because it was quicker than plucking it, soaked it in salt water overnight and roasted it with apples and onions. He had gathered cress salad from the island. The kitchen smelled like the best of ancient caves, Henry said. He did say that this wedding was not exactly the wedding he had planned. As they all knew, he had thought he would have it at Whitfield. Her second, his first, but he was happy, *very*, to be in this one, to be one of the principals. He did not say "and not be the best man," but maybe he was thinking it—not meaning that he was a better man than Jeremy, not best in that sense, but glad that this time he was not just the best man in the ceremony. This time, he was the groom, the happy groom.

This time, Laura is a very different bride, *very*.

The Brightleys, the only guests, brought japonica just in blossom, some of the brick red thorny sprays, from their yard. Alma put arm loads of it in old crocks on the porch and in the hall. The new minister at the Methodist church who had started visiting Gram agreed to conduct the ceremony—her first in a kitchen—but said she could not stay afterwards for the wild turkey and wedding cake because she had a funeral that afternoon.

Hill Brightley has traced back a connection to Jeremy's family. "We go back a long way. Excuse the joke, but we are old as the hills, me, that is, not my Alma, forever young, but not as the poet says, 'all breathing human passion far above,' and now I know that Jeremy is connected, way back, to us, distant, but connected. But most of all, he acted like, from what you have said, the young men in my family. Could have been first cousin to the one we called Wild Wystar. Hills are known for their tempers and crazinesses. We call it 'fire,' and I am sorry to say Jeremy lived up to the family stories. I come from a long line of hotheads. And most of the stories I know are, like this one: love stories. Wildness for a woman, we call it. Don't get me started telling stories. Wild Wystar hitchhiked across the country to see a girl he had met once, got to Oregon I believe it was, and found her, stayed for dinner, probably broke her heart (we are all of us heart breakers) and hitchhiked home. He was there three hours. If I get started telling stories, I'll stay for the honeymoon. Alma keeps me straight—on the straight and narrow, but I am a Hill, and could go off at any time, even with Alma here." Hill's blue eyes, his white hair, his goodness radiating from his shoulders as he hunches down in the rocking chair, make them laugh, thinking that he may go wild at any moment.

Alma takes his hand, "I am watching you."

They say that they plan to visit Jeremy's parents later in the spring and have every hope that by summer they will be having them come over. It may take time, but that's what they have plenty of.

Henry's father does not come to the wedding. Henry had told him he never wanted to see him again after that evening in February when Henry had gone to tell him that he was getting married soon, as soon as Laura could after the baby was born. But Henry's mother drove over to the wedding and helped wash dishes after the ceremony and the wild turkey feast. "James will regret not being here. I know him very well, but it was best that he not come, not yet."

Laura is flushed, weak, but "up and moving," she says, explaining her recovery by saying that grief is part of her motivation to get things going. Excited, if that is the word. "Phistic," really is the word, Henry keeps saying. Hyper, out of their minds, all of them. Henry is calling her Lazi, short for Lazarus, back from the dead, because she is: recently arrived, just off the boat, he says. A Persephone, a Eurydice who has, in spite of the command of the gods, come back from the jaws of death or the hell they had all been living in until she took up her pallet, so to speak, walked on down the line into the bright light.

And now, she has said she is marrying Henry! This is an announcement, not an explanation.

"None needed or requested," Henry says. "Let's do it."

Laura does recount for them, at least in part, what she plans to tell Henry's father later in the spring if he will listen. She will tell the back of his head if he turns his back on her. She practices what she will say. Her story will go like this:

After Rebecca and Weldon and Henry had left her— even Gram had gone away—on that December night, going out to the Rivanna Restaurant in their brave, pitiful hope of shocking her back into reality or life, and after Alma and Hill started visiting her every day, all day and some nights, talking about their Kelly, talking, talking for hours, she sat up, then got up. Not all at once, but slowly, not too surely, but finally, she got up. It was simple, that part, rising from the dead.

After she got up, she ate, she walked, she listened; in

short, as Henry said, she came back to life. Kelly Brightley brought her back—in a way—or her mother and father had. Laura could see, they all could, right there in front of them, true love. The Brightleys. Not just for each other, but for Kelly, not interrupted, hardly disturbed in its direction—this is the hard part to understand and demands many efforts at explanations—by Kelly's death. This true love is exactly what Laura had been trying to tell Rebecca and Weldon, trying to bring about in her own life, or in Rebecca and Weldon's: something about the fact that separation or loss does not necessarily break things up. Hovering over all of them, and especially Laura, the Brightleys, living proof of, and here was another hard part, the calculus, the slope to figure, Laura says. "Exactly." She had tried to love truly, to make things right with Henry and Jeremy. To love both of them. To glue them, the three of them (four with the baby) together in spite of the accident, but it was the wrong glue, and she had made the wrong calculations.

Alma says that it all takes time—the calculus, to use Laura's words, is slow, the slope long. She tells them that Hill collapsed when Kelly was killed and had taken it out on Weldon, demanding that he resign from teaching, write the terrible letter of confession to the school board. Hill can see it now and would do things differently, but he could not have acted any differently then for the world.

"It was the best he could do at the time," Alma says.

Laura will tell Henry's father about Kelly, about Dennis Johnson, so that he can understand how the Brightleys figure into their lives.

"Go ahead, try. You have worked miracles, so I don't it past you, but I can tell you, your work is cut out for you,"

Henry is smiling only about ten degrees when he says this.

Crazy sounding, she says, but it felt great, like a year of treatment at Lourdes, to feel Alma and Hill's love for Kelly going on and on in new ways, post–mortemly. In short, Laura will say to Henry's father, again and again if need be, that she got out of bed, had her baby, and married Henry. And she will write to Mr Moorefield, before and after the wedding and every week for the rest of their lives, so he will have every opportunity of knowing his granddaughter. Henry's father will know every detail and she wants him to know how it all happened, not that she can explain it, but she can try. She will start at a different point each time, one time telling him how the DNA from the band of the baseball cap in the ravine identified Jeremy. The report from the state lab had come in late January.

Henry is beside himself with his wedding coming so quickly—he had given it a year to happen at the quickest—and when Laura said they would get married on March twenty-third, he got very quiet, which is a sign of a deep idea settling in with Henry. And so, immediately, he had gone to tell his parents about the plans: one, two, three; baby, wedding, graduation. He had, of course, not been able to graduate in December. Now it would be May. Boom, boom, boom. Boom is right.

The news went over like a bomb. His father was terrible—he said Henry should have a paternity test made. How would Henry know that the baby was his, how would he know that he was not giving his life to another man's child. Wasn't his arm enough?

Henry said he simply nodded yes all through his father's raging questions. Yes, he wanted to have Jeremy's child, if the child were Jeremy's. It did not matter because the child was Laura's. Period. Besides, he loved Jeremy, had loved him, yes, had given, in a way, his arm for his friend, and he had loved Laura since the moment he saw her and more every minute of life. Yes, he wanted to marry Jeremy's wife, his widow, more than anything. Yes, as a matter of fact, or of soon–to–be-legal record, the baby was his. There would be adoption papers drawn up, kept in a safe, and if the baby at any point in her beautiful life, or her mother in hers, wanted the papers to go through, by God, they would. At this point, now, the baby, Elizabeth James Hill, was, *pace* DNA, his own. Then he had told his father he never would see him again until he changed his mind. At that point, he would welcome him home, the prodigal father.

Weldon thought that he himself filled those prodigal father shoes, that role.

"No more, nevermore, Father–in–law–to–be," Henry had said, not smiling.

Mr Moorefield is not as terrible as Henry thinks that he is, Laura tells them. Not as terrible as she herself has been, not as terribly mistaken. How would Henry feel, she asks, if Elizabeth, God forbid, should lose her arm on a dare. That brings the conversation down like a parachute floating to silence.

This spring and this summer she will go to see Mr Moorefield. She knows Henry's mother will want them to bring Elizabeth over, she says they are to come and not mind James who will come around eventually. She had come over to see Laura and Elizabeth the day they got home from the hospital, brought Henry's christening dress, laughed with Henry over how she and the baby had the same hair as her own—not much.

This spring, this summer, Laura will explain everything

to Henry's father. She hurries to correct herself, not explain adequately, but tell everything she knows. She thinks that when he hears everything in order, in a list, and starting at different points in the story, he may feel different about what Henry has done—married her—different about her and the baby.

Laura will tell him exactly how when the news came from the state lab that Jeremy was dead, identifying the remains the hunter found, she had been at the point of death herself, of taking her life, a process she had carefully planned as she lay all those months in bed. Of course, he knows about Jeremy's death, but she will begin with the report, there, though that is not the beginning. And of course, he knows that too.

She will tell him how much Jeremy had wanted to do something, anything—at least, she thought he meant *anything*—to make up for Henry's losing his arm, not that anything could bring it back, not that Henry ever blamed Jeremy, not that Henry even seemed to miss his arm, not as much as his father did as if he had lost his own arm. Mr Moorefield must know that all this is the truth.

Then Laura will tell him again how much they, she and Jeremy, both of them, wanted to do something for Henry. They felt that way, exactly the same, about wanting to think of some way to make amends, to compensate for his arm, not that they could, not that anything could, well, *pay*.

That was where she had gone wrong, thinking that she could help Jeremy do something for Henry. And so she—and she knows how this will sound—made a secret plan, a deal with herself: to have Henry's baby. No, she did not tell Henry what she was doing. That night on the island, out in the river, Henry thought she had changed her mind about marrying Jeremy, and that he was beginning the long love affair of his life, that the sex in the river on the old bridge piling was the beginning of their life together. She explains what she will tell Henry's father, and Henry listens to his favorite story—his "bedtime favorite" he says—they all listen, anticipating Henry's father's hearing the story, trying to take some of the shock out of it for him.

Laura had counted on Henry's natural instincts, his healthy ego and his sense of fate and his love, to make love at the river, no questions asked, all problems with facts—his best friend's bride-to-be—dissolving in the July darkness. Then when she told Henry that she was marrying Jeremy, not him, he made sense of it by thinking that she was feeling so guilty about hurting Jeremy that she was going ahead with the wedding. That's when Henry had demanded that the wedding be at Whitfield. It was the least he could do, he said. He blackmailed (call it by any other name) Laura. The wedding went forward, Mr Moorfield watching everything through the window, not knowing—no one but Laura knew that she was pregnant—not understanding why this wedding was being held at his home. This is the point where Henry's father will recall and enter the account personally, or not enter, but stand by the window, watching the groom, the young man he had wanted to have charged with the attempted murder of his son, the one-armed dancing fool out there spouting poetry and picking the bride's mother up from the floor where she has just fallen.

No, Laura will answer Henry's father's unspoken question, she never had sex again with Henry after that one time—until their wedding, and not then, of course, because she had just had a baby. It will be a hard story for him to listen to, she knows, but she will go on.

Henry had calmed down enough by that first wedding, enough to see things Laura's way, "through a glass darkly," he had said. She would have two children with Jeremy, he would be their Uncle Henry, all the things he was spouting at the wedding. He had no idea of the fact of the baby at the wedding. No knowledge of the baby he later called his Anne, the baby he thought would be born to Laura and Jeremy and that he would adopt ten years from then. And Jeremy did not know Laura was pregnant. Yes, she will say to James Moorefield, looking him straight in the eye, across the years of the generation, yes, she had been having sex with Jeremy for two years. The baby might be Jeremy's. It might be Henry's. She intended for the baby to be Henry's that night in July, but now she thinks of the baby as belonging to herself and to all of them. She will tell Henry's father how she waited until that night in the mountains, to tell Jeremy what she had done—to lock everything into place, and start their life off with the absolute truth. She was thinking that when Jeremy heard what she had done to make things right, trying to make things better for all of them, that he would feel such a wave of relief not just for Henry, but for himself, relief that he could be the old Jeremy, himself, his old self. He would have his life back, and laid out for him—he loved plans—written in stone. He and Laura had that in common, one of the many things. Jeremy could go ahead and work himself to death to give the child everything. Laura thought that she was helping Henry and Jeremy and herself, all of them. Deep in her deepest heart, that is what she thought. Henry's baby for Henry's arm. Something like that.

Now she knows that she was wrong. If Henry's father knew her better or at all, he would know how she has crossed a river. Yes, she was wrong. She will be crying by then. Yes, she made everything worse.

When she got home, walking and hitchhiking home from the honeymoon in the mountains, she began seeing that if it were not for her none of these bad things would have happened, not the arm, not the baby, not Jeremy's losing his mind and blowing up the car. She will be seeing things the way Henry's father sees them. That is when she had begun thinking in another wrong direction: if she could just get rid of herself, that would fix things. She did a pretty good job, she will tell him.

She did almost take herself out of the picture. Then, even that simple suicide plan got out of control. She saw, not too clearly, that she was doing something worse. Not simplifying things for other people, but complicating things. Dying does not make things simple.

Laura will tell Henry's father that she knows he wants a paternity test. She knows that when he told Henry this, that Henry cursed him and walked out.

When Henry had come back to Laura with this news, it was at this point that she got up from her death bed, not in a miraculous way, but slowly, Alma Brightley's arms around her. And so he, Mr James Moorefield, has saved her life, or helped save it with his son and her parents and the Brightleys, like it or not. And, she will tell Henry's father that he will have to know about Kelly Brightley and get to know her parents. He will have to know.

Even if Henry's father is not speaking to her, not even looking at Elizabeth, she will be speaking to him and will continue to speak to him, on the phone, in letters (emailing him if he will ever get a computer) forever, because he saved her life as much in a way as Alma and Hill Brightley had, as much as Rebecca and Weldon, as Gram, as Henry.

She will be repeating herself. His anger and his demand for the paternity test got her on her feet, saved her life and Elizabeth's. His terrible suggestion to have the baby tested, that was what made Laura want to make him understand, made her want to explain things, to get up. She knows how obnoxious her explanations are, and have been,

"And will be. Thank God," Henry interjects.

About the author

Susan Pepper Robbins lives in rural Virginia where she grew up. Her first novel was published when she was fifty ("One Way Home," Random House, 1993). Her fiction has won prizes (the Deep South Prize, the Virginia Prize) and has been published in many journals. Her collection of stories "Nothing But The Weather" was published in 2014. She teaches writing at Hampden-Sydney College.

Acknowledgements

I owe great thanks to Robert Peett for his careful and intuitive editing and his advice about the book at many stages, and to my brother W.E. Pepper, Jr. for his photograph used for the cover, and whose home, Elkora, was the setting for a beautiful and happier wedding than the one in this story. There are others whose help has been greater than they know , and they are listed here: Atalissa, Margaret and Lou, Maria, Rosalind, Sally, Lindsay, Amanda and Jim, Janet and Cameron, Mary and Bob, Diana, Jane, Frances and Alex, Deborah, and Richard, with special thanks to Michael Knight. My friends, students, and former students from Hampden-Sydney College have been wonderful.

My deep gratitude goes to my husband Roy and to our sons and their families. My nephews and nieces are treasures.